"I'm sorry I scared you," Patricio said, holding tightly to her hand.

His actions shocked her into silence. No one touched her—at least not unless it was under the orders of a director. But the people who worked for and around her always kept a respectful distance.

So when Patricio took her hand, even though it was obvious he was just inspecting it for damage or redness, it took her breath away.

You don't know him. And he doesn't even like you, she reminded herself. But she couldn't seem to pull away. He kept running his fingers along her skin, and all she could do was feel.

"Patricio," she murmured.

He went completely still, only his incredible, unreadable eyes moving upward to look her in the face. Light hit the scar above his eyebrow and she noticed it was more jagged and severe than she'd previously thought. He stared at her for a moment, and his expression changed. He was so close to her, and he looked...

Hungry. And heaven help her, she felt it, too.

SHADOW GUARDIAN
TRACY MONTOYA

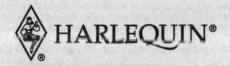

HARLEQUIN®

TORONTO • NEW YORK • LONDON
AMSTERDAM • PARIS • SYDNEY • HAMBURG
STOCKHOLM • ATHENS • TOKYO • MILAN • MADRID
PRAGUE • WARSAW • BUDAPEST • AUCKLAND

For Jose, as always. Love you.

ISBN 0-373-88663-2

SHADOW GUARDIAN

www.eHarlequin.com

Printed in U.S.A.

ABOUT THE AUTHOR

Harlequin Intrigue author Tracy Montoya is a magazine editor for a crunchy nonprofit in Washington, D.C., though at present she's telecommuting from her house in Seoul, Korea. She lives with a psychotic cat, a lovable yet daft Lhasa apso and a husband who's turned their home into the Island of Lost/Broken/Strange-Looking Antiques. A member of the National Association of Hispanic Journalists and the Society of Environmental Journalists, Tracy has written about everything from Booker Prize-winning poet Martín Espada to socially responsible mutual funds to soap opera summits. Her articles have appeared in a variety of publications, such as *Hope, Utne Reader, Satya, YES!, Natural Home,* and *New York Naturally.* Prior to launching her journalism career, she taught in an underresourced school in Louisiana through the AmeriCorps Teach for America program.

Tracy holds a master's degree in English literature from Boston College and a B.A. in the same from St. Mary's University. When she's not writing, she likes to scuba dive, forget to go to kickboxing class, wallow in bed with a good book or get out her new guitar with a group of friends and pretend she's Suzanne Vega.

She loves to hear from readers—e-mail TracyMontoya@aol.com or visit www.tracymontoya.com.

Books by Tracy Montoya

HARLEQUIN INTRIGUE
750—MAXIMUM SECURITY
877—HOUSE OF SECRETS*
883—NEXT OF KIN*
889—SHADOW GUARDIAN*

*Mission: Family

CAST OF CHARACTERS

Patricio Rodriguez—President of one of the best personal security companies in Los Angeles, Patricio's bodyguard services are much sought after. He doesn't get involved with clients' personal lives, but his inner demons guarantee that he'll protect them at all costs, even if he has to die doing it.

Sadie Locke—The Hollywood star is as low-maintenance and low-profile as an A-list actor can be in the City of Angels, but her need for independence is put to the test by an obsessed fan whose letters and phone calls are becoming increasingly violent.

Sonia Sanchez—Patricio watched her die at the hands of a violent street gang to which he belonged. Though it's been years since her death, Patricio is still haunted by her memory.

Lovesick—An obsessed fan whose fantasies about Sadie Locke make him believe they have a relationship where none exists. Through phone calls and letters, he's made it clear he'll do anything to possess her, even if he has to kill her.

Meghan Reilly—Sadie's personal assistant, and the closest thing she has to a friend. Will Meghan's loyalty cost her her life if she gets in Lovesick's way?

Cary Rhoades—He'll do anything to protect his girlfriend, Meghan, even if it means shadowing her to work and back.

Jack Donohue—Sadie's costar on the hit television show *Jungle Raider,* the action star is afraid of his own shadow in real life. Or is his timidity all an act?

Bobby Hayes—The hypercritical *Jungle Raider* director is torn between keeping his star safe and keeping his show on the air.

Daniel Rodriguez—Patricio's identical twin and a detective with the LAPD, Daniel has long been aware that his brother has a death wish. He'll do everything in his power to keep Patricio out of harm's way.

Prologue

Patricio was standing alone on his balcony when they came for him.

A glass of Jack Daniel's in his hand, he stared out at the lights of Los Angeles, spread out and twinkling against the shadowy silhouettes of the Hollywood Hills. He wasn't drunk yet, but maybe that didn't matter anymore.

It was quiet up here on the fifteenth floor, the sounds of blaring horns, pounding music and talking people muted by his distance from them. So even if he weren't on his guard, it still wouldn't have been difficult to hear the snick of the front door as it opened behind him, the soft footfalls on the carpet, though they tried to make no sound.

He tipped his glass to his mouth, the last of the whiskey burning his throat before he set the tumbler down on the small table beside him. There were five of them.

He sensed them creep closer, but still he didn't turn around. Not even when he felt the muzzle of a gun pressed against his neck, heard the sharp slide and click of the clip.

"Check it," an accented voice snarled in the darkness. "You can come with us, or I can shoot you where you stand. Your choice, *ese*."

His choice. Patricio didn't look at the speaker, though he knew it was O.T. Mejia. Old friend, old brother. Now, his friend wanted him dead or wanted him gone. Patricio's choice, and he didn't give a damn which way the wheel turned.

Seconds ticked by, until O.T. broke the silence with a sharp intake of air. Patricio felt the gun muzzle tremble against his temple, and then O.T. pushed it harder against his skin. "Dammit, Rico," O.T. said, a note of something Patricio had never heard from the man before creeping into his voice. "Don't make me do this."

Patricio kept his focus on the hills before them and remained silent. He wondered what it would be like to float over those hills, looking down at everyone and everything below as a dispassionate observer. He wondered if he'd ever find that kind of peace, in this life or the next.

Something slammed into his shoulder, and it wasn't until he fell against the rough stucco of the wall behind him that he realized it was O.T. who had shoved him backward. Patricio kept his hands at his sides, adjusting his balance so he was leaning casually against the wall as if nothing had happened. Keeping his expression neutral, he finally met his old friend's glare.

O.T. swiped at his nose with the sleeve of his red and black jacket, as close to losing it as he'd ever seen the man. "What's the matter with you, man?" O.T. asked, his voice shaking. Still holding the gun, he shoved Patricio again with both hands, the gun's muzzle pointed momentarily upward underneath Patricio's jaw. "What the hell's the matter with you?"

A brief vision of Sonia Sanchez, a curvy

girl with straight black hair and tight jeans, standing alone as nine men formed a circle around her flashed through Patricio's mind.

His focus still on O.T., Patricio made a peace sign, curving his fingers forward slightly, and brought the sign of the Almighty Latin Cobra Nation over his heart.

O.T. blinked, brought the gun down to his side.

The shadows behind him seemed to sigh with relief.

And then Patricio threw it down, shaking the sign off his hand as if it were something dirty, perverse. Maybe it was, maybe it always had been.

Throwing down the sign of the Cobras was the highest insult he could have given the group before him, and he knew it. So again, he waited.

"You disrespecting us? Are you disrespecting us?," he heard Jaybird Alvarez snarl as he stepped forward, his angular face illuminated by the city lights. "Finish it, O.T., or I'll finish him for you."

"Yes, O.T.," Patricio said mockingly,

speaking for the first time since the Cobras had arrived. "Finish it." *Finish me.*

Another too-vivid memory, this one of Sonia begging King Cobra Antonio "Tone" Vicente to be initiated into the Cobra Nation. Of her choosing a "beating in" rite. Of eight men circling her, while Patricio had been too wasted to do more than stumble along the perimeter, slurring at them to leave her alone. Of eight men delivering brutal blows with their fists, their boots. Of Sonia crumpling to the ground. Of a flash of glass from a broken bottle.

And then the eight men had disappeared, leaving only Patricio to watch the pool of blood under Sonia's neck slowly grow larger, until it coated her hair, the soles of his boots, his clothes.

His hands.

Finish me, dammit.

"You heard the man," another Cobra growled in the darkness. "He's begging for it, O.T."

"Shut up," Mejia whispered, staring at the gun in his hand.

"Freaking do it already!" another said.

O.T.'s head snapped up. "Shut up!" he shouted. He brought the gun up and swung his outstretched arm around in a semicircle, effectively getting the Cobras that had been breathing down his neck for a kill to back off.

"The Cobra Nation is done, O.T.," Patricio said to his old friend's back. "It's over."

"Screw you, Rico." O.T. turned back to Patricio, the gun pointed at his heart. With a lunge, he slammed his body against Patricio's, knocking him once more against the wall. Gripping a fistful of material from Patricio's T-shirt, O.T. shoved the gun under his jaw. "There's still a Cobra Nation tonight," he hissed. "And if you're going to leave it, you're going to leave it my way."

He curved his arm out and delivered a backhand swing, the pistol and O.T.'s fist connecting squarely with Patricio's jaw. And then, all Patricio saw was darkness.

LATER—whether it was several hours or several days later, he didn't know—Patricio woke to find himself on a cold, concrete floor. His head ached like a bitch, and his mouth tasted like blood.

Light from the street lamps outside filtered through the broken windows, illuminating specks of dust that danced through the air. He knew this place—one of the most senior Cobras had bought the place on Tremont Street for those belonging to the Marengo and Soto Streets section of the East L.A. Cobras. It served as a safe house to hide from the cops, a temporary storage unit for the illegal substances that formed most of the gang's income, and a place to hold meetings when secrecy and isolation were a necessity. If they were going to do this at the warehouse, he was in trouble.

Bracing his hands underneath him, Patricio pushed his torso up. Before he could stand, a figure melted out of the darkest corners of the warehouse and slowly walked toward him, his footsteps echoing softly on the concrete. Then another stepped forward, and another, until the room was full of Cobras, forming a circle around him.

Forgetting about his aching head, Patricio pushed himself up to standing, determined to get to his feet before they could kick him back down. As soon as he was upright and steady, O.T. moved beside him in the center of the circle. He didn't look at Patricio.

"For those of you who don't know him, this brother is Rico Rodriguez. He's been a brother for many years, and he's a Cobra wherever he stands," O.T. intoned, moving slowly to face all members of the circle as he spoke. "We, the Latin Cobras of Marengo and Soto have been designated by King Cobra Tone to deal with the breaking of our laws."

"This brother is becoming an alcoholic. He was wasted when he tried to halt a Cobra High Initiation Rite, and he has disrespected his fellow brothers." Murmurs of assent from the crowd surrounding them greeted O.T.'s words. The Cobras had probably killed hundreds of rival gang members in just the past year, but they had their own bizarre moral code. Being a lush was not looked upon well. "He will receive a three-minute head-to-toe violation, or he will be violated out of the Cobras," O.T. continued. "His choice."

O.T. turned to face Patricio, eye to eye. "It's your choice, Rico," he said softly.

A violation meant that every man in the room would be allowed to beat Patricio, as hard as he wanted, and in any way he could manage, from head to toe until O.T. called time. Under Cobra law, Patricio couldn't fight back and keep his honor—and to be without honor inside this circle would be his funeral.

If he chose three minutes, he would be back in the good graces of the Cobras after it was all over. If he chose to be violated out of the gang, they'd leave him alone after all was said and done, and he'd be out. The catch was, O.T. could let the beating go on as long as he wanted, even long after Patricio was dead. Last time a Cobra had chosen to be violated out, he'd ended up in a coma for over a month.

Someone cracked his knuckles, the snaps reverberating throughout the room. "I want out," Patricio said.

Mentally prepared though he was, the first blow caught him by surprise, knocking the air out of him. Almost immediately, the second connected with his still-tender jaw, causing him to briefly lose consciousness. He awoke seconds later on the cold ground, bursts of pain erupting on his chest, his head, neck, shoulders, legs, back. Not a sound escaped his lips, and he didn't lift a finger to defend himself. Not even when they broke his ribs.

Exactly three minutes after it had started, O.T. called time.

His chest burning with a searing, knife-like pain every time he moved, Patricio pushed himself up on his hands and knees, gasping for air. Pausing to steady himself, he closed his eyes briefly, then stood. He wrapped his arm around his left side. Every square inch of his body felt like raw meat, and blood ran into his eyes from the blows he'd taken to his head. His world was spinning, and he didn't know if he could stand for more than a minute, didn't know if he'd even be able to crawl his way out of the warehouse.

"Don't stand!" someone shouted. "Don't you dare stand, you mother—"

Patricio's hand snapped up, catching the fist that had come flying toward his face as if it were a baseball. He squeezed, putting pressure on the tenderest parts of his attacker's hand, until the man made a sound, an "ahhh" of pain. Patricio remembered that hand, remembered how it had held a piece of glass, glinting in the light, slicing through the air toward Sonia's bare neck.

"Don't touch me," Patricio said, his voice low and so soft, several men moved to hear him. "Don't you ever touch me again."

The room was thick with dust and silence, until O.T. finally stepped forward, making a gesture of dismissal. Several seconds ticked by, and then the men started falling back, until there was only Patricio and O.T. left.

Something like regret in his brown eyes, O.T. brought the curved peace sign to his heart. *"Paz,"* he said. Peace.

Patricio waited for the rest of the familiar greeting, the familiar goodbye. "*Paz* to the Almighty Latin Cobra Nation."

But O.T. just said, "Peace, brother," and then he, too, slipped away into the darkness.

Chapter One

Twelve years later

Sadie Locke clung to the landing struts of the helicopter as it rose above the Inca ruins of Macchu Picchu, past the point of no return where she could have jumped to safety. Her arms aching, she swung her legs upward, but the helicopter lurched abruptly, and she was unable to wrap them around the strut. Her lower body fell once more, jolting her shoulders so they felt they were going to come out of their sockets.

"God, I hate heights," she muttered through gritted teeth, closing her eyes tightly in an effort to prevent herself from looking down at the increasingly tiny ruins and lush green cliffs below her. The wind tore at her short brown hair, blowing the long top layers wildly around her face as the chopper blades whirred loudly above her.

Just then, she sensed something that made her open her eyes again. A light-skinned blond man, dressed in a loose-fitting shirt and pants of Peruvian cotton, had spotted her from inside the chopper. He waved his gun in her direction, shouting something to the people behind him. Around his neck was a dazzling ruby, suspended on a gold chain. The Jewel of Amarra.

But it wasn't the jewel she was after, not this time. "Tate!" she shouted, knowing as she did so that no one in the chopper could hear her over the *whomp-whomp* of the blades. Tightening the elbow of her right arm around the strut to better support herself, she skimmed her left hand down the hip of her cargo shorts until it reached the holster strapped around her thigh.

Empty. Her gun had probably become a permanent part of the Peruvian landscape during their ascent.

Before she could think about what she was doing, Sadie looked down, as if she could spot the gun from that high up. "Nice," she murmured as the landscape sped by below her.

The chopper dipped suddenly, and Sadie reached up to wrap her left hand back around the strut just in time. The man above her stumbled against the open door frame, almost falling forward but then regaining his balance and his equilibrium. Sadie saw him shout something to the pilot, and then the helicopter evened out, making a smooth path over the Andes Mountains.

With a grunt, Sadie swung her legs upward again, crossing the ankles of her brown hiking boots around the other end of the strut. She heaved herself up and around the strut so her stomach was resting on it, then reached up to grab the bottom of the doorway in which the man with the gun was standing for support.

The man grinned at her, leveling his gun at her head.

Pulling up so she was kneeling on the strut, Sadie delivered a backhand chop to the man's knee. He fired a wild shot that missed her by a mile. As his leg buckled, she gripped his pant leg and yanked him toward her. His feet went out from under him, and, arms flailing, he tumbled out of the helicopter....

...and onto a blue stunt mat two feet below.

"And that's a wrap," Bobby Hayes, *Jungle Raider's* director called out. The giant fans next to the helicopter stopped humming as the crew shut their motors down, though their blades kept whirring in slow circles.

"Locke, you look tired," Bobby said, chomping down on an obscenely large wad of Bazooka gum. He must have shoved at least three pieces into that wide, gap-toothed mouth of his. "Get some rest. We'll start shooting episode one-seven-five on Monday." He pointed at two burly crewmen and smacked down on his gum a couple more times before booming, "DeFazio, Mellencamp, help her down. She breaks a leg getting off that thing, we're all out of a job."

Sadie was sorely tempted to jump off the helicopter—which was suspended from the high ceiling by thick cables—herself. Just to raise Bobby's blood pressure a little in return for the comment about her looks. But the gaffer and the lighting tech beat her to the punch, flanking her on either side and taking her arms to help her gently to the ground.

"You heard the man, Sadie," the taller of the two said to her. "Can't have our star breaking her neck on a two-foot jump. My wife would kill me if I lost this gig." He winked at her.

"That'd be bad," she agreed. "Thanks, Tom." The two men continued to hold her elbows until she'd bounded across the puffy blue mat and was safely on the concrete floor of the studio building. "How's that little girl of yours, Martin?" The lighting technician and his wife had adopted a baby daughter from China, and he'd only recently gotten back from family leave.

"Aw, she's something else," Martin replied, a grin that could only be described as goofy blossoming on his full-cheeked face.

"Yesterday, she came crawling over when I walked in from work, and she actually pulled herself up on my pantleg until she was standing."

Sadie had to laugh at the big man's face—nothing like a new baby girl to turn a macho man into Jell-O. "Enjoy it, Martin. I hear it goes fast. But don't you dare think of leaving again for a while. Nobody else can take ten years off my face the way you can." Though her tone was joking, she was totally serious. A great lighting tech was worth his or her weight in gold to any actress older than thirty.

Martin ran a hand across his silver and brown crew cut. "Sadie, you don't need no lighting to look good. My wife always says she'd kill for your cheekbones."

Sadie smiled her thanks at the compliment. "Tell Nina I'll have to show her some of the tricks they do in the makeup trailer sometime. Take care, you two." She gave them a cheery wave and walked off the set, trying not to show how bone-tired she was until she was safely outside. These all-nighter wrap-up shoots were getting more and more difficult the older she got. It was 6:00 a.m., and it felt like she hadn't slept or eaten since last week.

As she headed for the studio parking lot, Meghan Reilly, her assistant, fell into step beside her. "So you've got a cover shoot at seven-thirty for *Mystique* magazine—they want you in leopard-print, sorry about that. At least I talked them out of the exploitative bikini." Meghan took a deep breath now that her first volley of words was out, looking fresh and rested as ever. Most likely because she was fresh and rested— Sadie had sent her home yesterday afternoon—while Sadie herself felt like she'd been run over by a convoy of tourist-toting Franklin Studios golf carts. Twice.

"Then we have a brief interview with Maxine Winter from *Entertainment This Week* to promote the two hundredth episode," Meghan continued. "It's right across the street. After that, I'll give you your laptop with the satellite hookup in the limo, and you can do that quick chat with Hollyweird.com. We have the Girls, Inc., charity luncheon at one at the Biltmore. You'll smile, accept their Role Model Girl of the Year award, eat the rubber chicken and then we'll leave. We'll have you back in the studio for those voice dubs you need to do this afternoon, and then I have Joaquin Ferrer and his minions coming over to do your hair and makeup for the MTV Movie Awards tonight. Do you still want to wear that vintage Valentino, because Dolce & Gabbana sent over this amazing tangerine sheath for you—?"

Meghan finally paused to take another breath, and Sadie decided to take advantage of it. "I'm not going." The woman had only been her assistant for three weeks, but Sadie already knew how much Meghan was going to love that statement.

"What?" The petite redhead squeaked, coming to a halt in the middle of the Franklin Brothers Studio parking lot. Her large, chin-length curls kept on going a second longer than she had, then bounced back into place. "You can't skip! You're nominated for—" Sadie kept walking, and she heard Meghan's shoes scuffle against the blacktop as the woman scrambled to catch up.

"I'm not going," Sadie reiterated once Meghan was at her side once more. "Please send the dress back to Domenico and Stefano with my deepest thanks, but—"

"You're on a first-name basis with Dolce & Gabbana?" When Sadie didn't respond, Meghan rolled her eyes at herself. "Of course you are. Okay. Dress and deepest thanks to Domenico and Stefano." She opened her ever-present leather planner and took the pencil out of its little looped holder inside. "Do you think Domenico and Stefano would mind if I tried the dress on first? Paraded around the office for a minute?" she asked, scribbling a note to herself while she walked.

Sadie raised an eyebrow, a look she'd practiced in the mirror and usually had people scrambling to do whatever it was she wanted. Maybe it was her eyes—a blue so pale and icy that if she wasn't grinning like a maniac, she always looked aloof, if not downright peeved. So when she actually tried to look annoyed, the earth generally moved.

And once again, it worked, but maybe

too well. Meghan visibly recoiled, and Sadie almost regretted her harsh reaction. Almost. But years of television and movie fame had taught her the hard way that there was a glass wall between herself and the rest of the world. People loved her *Jungle Raider* character, not her, and they were invariably disappointed that she wasn't as funny or charming or kickass in person. Or, they swiftly figured out how useful it was to know a rich and famous person—you got into the best clubs, got the best tables at restaurants, rubbed elbows with other rich and famous people, found it easier to get your damn photos or music tapes or scripts in front of the right people. There was never any real affection on their part, no matter how good her intentions. It was always all about what she could do for them.

And it hurt, every time.

Sadie came to a halt in front of the small, palm-lined pond the studio had used for a couple of Sahara Desert oasis scenes in episode 168. The California sun beating down on her face and shoulders, she pinched the bridge of her nose, closing her eyes as the palms swished above her in the breeze.

"I'm sure they wouldn't even notice if you tried on the dress, Meghan," she said quietly. "You can have it, if you want."

Meghan gave her a wide, toothy grin with all the force of her natural exuberance behind it. And in Meghan's case, that was a lot of force. "I was kidding, boss. Tangerine doesn't work with my skin and hair, unless cadaverous is in nowadays." She snapped her planner closed and tucked it under one willowy arm. "But why are you skipping the MTV awards? Just tired, or is there something else I should know?"

Sadie opened her mouth and then closed it again, flipping her palms in the air and then shoving a hand through her short, dark hair, undoubtedly messing up the diagonal line of her once-perfect bangs. You know, it would be nice to just dive into that little pond and leave Meghan behind without having to explain things....

"It's Lovesick again, isn't it?" Meghan said softly, all the chirp gone from her voice.

The woman's perception bordered on

eerie sometimes. Sadie was about to protest that no, it was nothing, when her mind
shot back to last night's phone call—a call
that had come to her personal, unlisted
number at home. Just a creepy voice whispering "Saaaaaddiiiiiieeeeeee" over and
over again in a way that said his intentions
were far from innocent. She'd hung up,
and he'd called again and again until she'd
left the phone off the hook. And then her
cell phone had started ringing...

She must have looked terrified all over
again, because Meghan tucked an arm
around her and hustled her across the lot
to her Honda Civic Hybrid, parked in a
prime spot near a small sign with her name
on it. With the push of a button on her key
chain, Sadie unlocked the doors and got in
behind the wheel, with Meghan taking the
passenger seat. After the doors were
closed and locked, Meghan swiveled in
her seat to face her.

"Omigod, I knew those letters were getting too weird." She opened her planner
again and started extracting business cards
from the plastic cardholders in the back.

"Look, I know you don't want a body-guard, but I think it would be a good idea until we find out who this freak is. I went through and found some good security companies—"

"No."

Meghan looked up, business cards arranged under her nose like the fan of a Civil War-era debutante. "But—"

Sadie leaned against the driver's side door and crossed her arms in front of her chest. "Thanks, Meghan, but you're all the entourage I want right now."

Meghan let out her loud, barking laugh that invariably made anyone within earshot want to join her. Sadie remained silent.

"I need to put that in my résumé— 'Served as Sadie Locke's one-woman entourage from October to present. Duties included fawning, scraping, obsequious compliments, and the occasional spontaneous burst of applause.'" Dropping her planner and the cards into her lap, Meghan clapped her hands lightly but rapidly next to one cheek to illustrate.

Sadie frowned. "Meghan, I didn't mean—"

"I know, boss. You have to learn to take a joke."

Despite the fact that it was probably in her best interests to keep an emotional distance from her employees, she hadn't been able to stand it when Meghan had started calling her "Ms. Locke." She'd told her assistant to call her Sadie, but generally, Meghan defaulted to "boss" instead. Habit, she said, from when she'd worked for a "trampy little teenage rock star" who'd wanted Meghan to call her "ma'am." Ma'aming a fifteen-year-old had made Meghan bust out laughing every time she tried it, so she'd settled for "boss" instead, and all of her employers had been "boss" ever since.

Meghan held out her hand. "Why don't you give me the keys, and I'll get you to that *Mystique* shoot? You don't look so good."

Sadie picked her keys up from where she'd dropped them in her lap and toyed with the one for her Honda's ignition. You knew it was going to be a bad day when people couldn't stop telling you how awful you looked. "It's okay. I think I'll drive myself. You can just go back to doing whatever it is you do to keep my life running so well."

Meghan shot her a mother-knows-best look. "Are you sure you're in any shape to drive? You looked totally terrified a minute ago. I don't think you should be alone right now. What happened to that big, buff driver I heard you used to have?"

Well, Sadie had fired him after he'd sold a story about her "revolving bedroom door" to the *National Tattler,* that horrible gossip rag. And then she'd sued him for slander—for a public apology, not money—sued the paper for libel— for money, of course—and had given her entire settlement to charity. Just another case of how letting someone into her life had gone terribly, terribly wrong. Once upon a time, she'd loved their morning chats while he'd driven her to the studio, talking about his new granddaughter and his big Italian family. The creep.

"I like driving," she told Meghan. "Clears my mind."

A few minutes later, after a mini-barrage of protests and advice, Meghan departed, still muttering as she walked away but leaving Sadie alone inside her Civic all the same. After pressing the button to lock all four doors, Sadie put her key in the ignition and pushed an Arturo Sandoval Cuban jazz CD into the CD player. She leaned forward to rest her forehead against the steering wheel, closing her eyes and enjoying the strains of Sandoval's trumpet amid the driving beat of conga drums.

A tap on the passenger side window startled her into lifting her head and opening her eyes. An elderly man wearing a terrible Hawaiian shirt bent to peer through the glass, a wide, toothy smile on his face. He nodded his liver-spotted head happily while making a cranking motion with his hand, apparently trying to get her to roll down her window.

Her hand hovering over the button for the automatic windows, Sadie glanced at the expensive Nikon around his neck. Pa-

parazzi. Dammit, those studio tour guides were getting more and more lax about letting tourists wander off their little golf carts, and the vultures were taking notice. She shot the man an apologetic smile and hit the door locks again, just in case.

His own smile vanished in response, replaced by a scowl. But it wasn't the expression on his face that caused her blood to suddenly run cold, but the fawning, almost worshipful look in his eyes.

Oh, God.

He pulled a set of keys out of his shorts pocket.

Scrabbling for her own keys, Sadie turned them in the ignition and caused the already powered up engine to shriek in response. Dammit. Her hand went to the automatic gearshift, but not before she heard the sound of metal clicking against metal.

The door opened.

She put the car in Reverse, but the old man slipped into the passenger seat with a dexterity belying his years. She stomped on the brakes so hard, her body jerked tight against the seat belt, and the man had to brace himself on the dashboard. Sweat beaded on his temple, and she could see the waxy sheen of pancake makeup on his face, the faint line of latex prosthetic pieces covering his neck and head. The old man disguise might have fooled anyone who hadn't been in the business for years. It didn't fool her. Underneath the makeup, this guy was young. And strong.

He shut the door. She put the car in Park.

"What do you want?" she asked.

"Saaaadiiiieeee," he hissed in the same voice she'd heard on her unlisted phone the night before, an eerie, empty-eyed smile on his face.

Chapter Two

"I'm loooovesick," he said, still in the same eerie, high-pitched tone.

What were you supposed to do in a situation like this? Go along with the guy's fantasy? Be assertive and tell him to get the hell out of your car? Try to undo the seat belt without him noticing and bolt for the hills? What? What? Maybe if she followed her first impulse and threw up, he'd be so grossed out, he'd leave her alone for good.

"What do you want?" she asked again, her fingers moving to the catch of her seat belt. She could have bolted pretty successfully if it hadn't been for the device.

"You, Sadie. We're meant to be." Now his voice was somewhat normal, though he whispered the words, perhaps in another attempt to disguise himself. He reached forward and stroked her bare arm lightly with the back of his hand. "You're so beautiful," he whispered. "Such beautiful skin. I know how you like compliments."

She shrank back toward the door as subtly as she could. "How did you get my car keys?"

He kept stroking her skin. "You shouldn't leave your purse lying around on the set. Anyone could go through it. Anyone could make a copy of anything they wanted. You can't trust people nowadays. It's a good thing I'm here to look out for you." The too-long nail of his index finger sliced along the inside of her forearm, leaving a faint, white line in its wake.

Each breath caught in her throat as she tried not to gag, her inhalations coming out as hiccups. *God, don't touch me. Please stop touching me.* "You need to leave me alone." The car felt so small, so cramped, as if she were growing larger and it was closing in around her.

The man cocked his head to the side and gave her a knowing look, clucking his tongue. "Playing hard to get, Sadie? It won't work. I know you love me. We're meant to be."

He put a small bunch of violets on the dashboard, their stems wrapped together with a white, chiffon ribbon. "I brought you these. I know how much you like them. They're your favorite, aren't they?"

She looked away. They were her favorite, but she didn't remember ever telling anyone that.

Out of the corner of her eye, Sadie saw a studio security guard walking across the parking lot, a half-eaten doughnut in one hand. She unhooked her seat belt.

Next to her, her stalker reached into the pocket of his Bermuda shorts and pulled out a Swiss Army knife. He flicked what had to be the largest blade out of the handle with his thumb, then snapped it back in again.

Snap. The blade was out. Snap. The blade was in.

Oh, no....

Reaching under the steering wheel, Sadie pressed the button that activated the car alarm. Instantly the Civic was all flashing lights and strident horn blasts, the little car practically shaking with all the commotion it was creating.

"Nooo!" Just as she'd opened the driver's side door, he struck out with the backside of his closed fist, connecting with her temple. She felt a burst of pain on the side of her head, and then her world started fading away, the noises around her muffling as her vision tunneled. In one last effort to get away before her world collapsed inward, Sadie crumpled against the door and onto the blacktop.

"They're coming! They'll take you away from me!"

She could hear feet running as the world spun around her, but they sounded so far away.

"I'll see you again, Sadie," a voice whispered in her ear. She couldn't move, couldn't see. She willed her body to push the speaker away, but her arms felt so heavy.

"We'll be together forever. I know you love me. I'll make you remember you love me."

The last thing she felt was Lovesick's hot breath on her face. And then she lost consciousness.

"Unnnhh." Decidedly groggy, Sadie forced her eyes open, noting a handful of blurred, moonlike faces hovering over hers. She blinked several times in succession, finally managing to focus on one.

The man wore a white lab coat with a photo ID clipped to the collar telling the world his name was Tate Ashcroft, M.D. He had one of those little black ear, nose and throat lights in one hand, which he was attempting to shine in Sadie's eyes.

"Look up at the ceiling," he intoned in a deep, commanding voice.

"Knock it off, Jack," she said in speech that was only slightly slurred, pushing the light away from her face. "You're only a doctor on TV, remember? Or did you hit your head, too?" Reaching behind her, she lightly rubbed the back of her skull, which was sore to the touch and had a large bump that seemed to be growing by the second.

He twisted the light in his large, tanned

hands, looking more than a little hurt. "I've been Dr. Tate Ashcroft for seven years. That's more than enough time for me to have learned something."

"Okay, out of the way. Step back. Step back. There's nothing to see here." Meghan pushed her way through the small crowd that had gathered and crouched down to where Sadie was still sitting on the pavement. "Down, Jack," she said without turning her head to the actor hovering behind her, apparently still hoping he might be of some assistance.

Meghan leaned in and whispered to Sadie, "Are you okay? I didn't want to call an ambulance, because this would be all over the papers, so I brought in my doctor. She's a big fan. And her office is next to the studio." Meghan gestured to a slim, tall brunette leaning against Meghan's Ford Escort, a designer satchel in one hand. The woman adjusted her expensive sunglasses and acted nonchalant, bless her, as if she visited studio lots all the time.

Jack was still hovering around when Dr. Marin Vega, a real doctor of medicine, thank goodness, started packing her things in her Murakami for Louis Vuitton bag. After informing Sadie that she only had a mild concussion, Dr. Vega told her what symptoms to keep an eye on and pre-scribed rest and some ice packs. Jack, on the other hand, looked like he wasn't sat-isfied.

"Sadie, how long have we been working together?" he asked, once the bona fide M.D. had left the scene.

Jungle Raider, their action-adventure television series, had been running for a good seven years now, with the occasional movie spinoff. Her character, Harvard Ph.D. Jada Winthrop, solved a new arche-ology-related mystery every week and usu-ally ran into more than her share of scrapes. Which had her running to her close friend and dig site medic Dr. Tate Ashcroft for bandages, advice, and ratings-boosting sexual tension. In real life, she wasn't even remotely attracted to Jack, but they were darn good at faking it.

"Long enough that my manager is giv-ing me names of plastic surgeons," she said, feeling a little less groggy now that she'd been sitting up for a while. "Why, Jack?"

"That was Lovesick, wasn't it?" When she didn't answer, he ran a hand along his light-brown hair, stopping just short of shoving his fingers through it and messing up his artfully arranged waves. "The security guard saw him in the car with you. Obviously this creep is starting to get gutsier. You need protection." He smacked his ear light against an open palm.

"That's what I've been telling her," Meghan interjected in her long-suffering Meghan way.

Sadie sighed. Jack may have been a little weird, but he was the closest thing she had to a friend. He'd read the first letter from Lovesick over her shoulder on set, and he'd heard all about the almost daily letters she'd gotten over the past several months, which had turned from fawning to fawning and vaguely threatening to fawning and outright psychotic.

"Jack, I don't need protection. I don't want someone in my space 24/7, okay?" Her voice was a little sharper than she'd intended.

"It's not bad. Trust me. I know a guy…."

"Jack." Meghan rifled quickly through her planner. "I think she needs someone who can protect her from more than kittens."

Jack had had a bad experience as a child with a pair of unneutered Siamese kittens. It had left its mark, and the man lived in fear of both the little furry creatures and word of his phobia leaking to the media. He could handle snakes, spiders and scorpions without batting an eye, at least most of the time, but kittens were a different story. He was an adult and an actor now—he could pretend they didn't bother him quite successfully if he had to—but a perceptive person could always tell that the action star got cold sweats from the tiny furballs.

"Low blow, Meg."

She grinned. "Thank you." She turned back to Sadie. "Look, boss, I'm serious. Lovesick's behavior is getting more violent. You need someone to watch over you, and I won't take no for an answer." She fanned out a selection of business cards in her right hand like a Vegas card dealer. "Pick a bodyguard. Any bodyguard."

Jack folded his arms across his gym-toned chest. "Patricio Rodriguez."

Meghan shot him a glare through the red curls that had tumbled down her forehead. "I'm not finished."

Jack shrugged. "He's the best. Professional. Effective. Invisible. Not to mention fearless. The man heli-skis off sixty-degree inclines on a dull day."

"Look, she needs a bodyguard, not G.I. Joe." Meghan flipped through some notes, then paused, raising her eyebrows. "Although he's on my short list of recommendations," she conceded. "Comes with a lot of excellent, A-list referrals."

"No," Sadie said with what she hoped was an air of finality. "I'll have my security company double-check my system at home, but that's all I'm—"

"He's discreet. He's worked for me off and on for the last five years." Jack curled his fingers inward toward his palm and made a show of studying his buffed nails. "He knows about the kittens."

Sadie raised an eyebrow, then stopped because even that movement hurt her head. Meghan patted Jack on the shoulder. "That's pretty darn discreet, boss." She closed her planner and tucked it back in her shoulder bag. "What if Lovesick comes back? What if he corners you where no one is there to see? The guard said his old man disguise would have been way convincing if it weren't for his record-breaking sprint out of here. A man with that kind of talent at hiding his identity?" She shuddered. "He could be anyone. Anywhere. One woman alone can't fend off an enemy she can't see."

Sadie rubbed her temples, the action not doing much for her pounding head. An enemy she couldn't see. That summed it up well, didn't it? And even Jada Winthrop, with her black belt in Aikido and her skill at throwing knives couldn't match up against an invisible foe with the element of surprise on his side.

PART OF HER unspoken agreement with Meghan—the one where she did what Meghan asked and Meghan stopped nagging her—was to agree to be ferried around the city by a limo service while the nearest Honda Service Center changed the locks on her Civic. And so there she was, sinking into the ridiculously plush back seat of a Rolls-Royce Silver Shadow with a Diet Coke in one hand, waiting for Meghan to come out of the tinted glass and black granite building that housed the offices of Rodriguez and Associates, among others.

Not that she was any bit happier with the idea of hiring a bodyguard. But it had only taken minutes for Bobby Hayes, *Jungle Raider*'s director, to hear through the Franklin Studios grapevine about what had happened and go into a full-fledged panic over the thought of his star in jeopardy. It had only taken one "offhand" remark from Meghan about hiring Sadie a bodyguard before Bobby had made it a mandate. Now, Sadie had forty-eight hours to find the perfect protection specialist before Bobby's "or else" came into effect. And knowing Bobby's penchant for overreacting, she'd end up with her own personal military platoon, complete with a tank and occasional F-16 flybys, if she didn't show up at work in two days trailing some kind of security contingent. Given what Jack had said about Patricio Rodriguez's discretion, Sadie figured he was the lesser of all of the evils whose business cards were in Meghan's planner.

After only a few short minutes inside Rodriguez's office building, Meghan came out, and she didn't look happy. "Would you believe it?" she asked as she got into the limo, promptly sinking into the interior. "Whoo! Plush seats." She hoisted herself upward and readjusted her body on the seat so it was no longer slumping into the cushion. "There's a waiting list. I told them who you were, and that pit bull of a secretary just kept repeating that Mr. Rodriguez and his associates had a lot of important people to protect and weren't interested in acquiring more clients at this time. And when I asked to speak to Mr. Rodriguez himself, the pit bull said he'd just gotten back from Ecuador and was not to be disturbed."

She bit her lip and looked at Sadie, and the two of them just sat for a moment in a companionable, defeated silence. Then, Meghan started shuffling through her collection of business cards once more. "I have other security specialist referrals. Their credentials weren't quite as impressive as Mr. Rodriguez's, but they're still amazing." She held up a light blue card. "Here's an ex-CIA agent with marksmanship qualifications. I think that means he's a sniper. Delmar Woodward—"

"Why was Rodriguez the most impressive? Other than the whole kittens thing with Jack?" Sadie asked. She didn't think much could beat an ex-CIA sniper.

Meghan expertly extracted Patricio Rodriguez's business card out of her planner, then pulled out her electronic personal digital assistant. "Downloaded their résumés into here last week." Meghan's organizational methods were a dizzying combination of electronic, paper and miscellaneous sticky notes, but somehow, she made it work. "Let's see." She tapped on the small screen with her stylus. "Former Delta Force operative. Well-versed…oh, excuse me. *Extremely* well-versed in personal protection, hand-to-hand combat, marksmanship, bomb detection, hostage negotiation and extraction, building assault, electronic surveillance and countermeasures, deadly weapons, crowd and perimeter control, evasive driving and the psychology of fear."

Whoa. "The psychology of fear?"

Meghan tucked the stylus behind one ear and started to fan herself with her hand. "Wow, I'm feeling a little flushed. On paper, this man is kinda hot. If I didn't already have a boyfriend…"

"Actually he sounds too scary to be true." Letting the rest of Meghan's words catch up to her, Sadie interrupted herself. "Wait, you have a boyfriend? When did this happen?" She worked so hard to keep her relationship with Meghan strictly professional, so it always came as a strange shock when Meghan's nonwork life came up. But of course she had a life outside work. Sadie was the one who didn't.

Meghan tilted her head and toyed with a lock of her red hair. "We met a few weeks ago at the Santa Monica Pier. I was stuffing a hot dog in my face, and I looked up and there he was!" She grinned. "I mean, it's still really new and everything, so he has plenty of time to turn into Jabba the Hutt the Human Slug, but right now, it's really great. He's a wannabe actor, of course. Who isn't in this city besides me?"

"You should bring him by the studio sometime. I'd like to meet him." Sadie immediately wanted to smack herself for saying that. Encouraging Meghan to be her friend as well as her assistant would only result in disaster. Or, at least, some really unflattering photos of her showing up in *US* magazine or a vicious tell-all in the *Enquirer*. She knew this, but she couldn't seem to stop herself.

Nor could she stop the damned warm fuzzy feeling she got when Meghan brightened visibly at the suggestion. "I'd love for you to meet him. Give me your thoughts." But then, she pulled the PDA stylus from behind her ear, using it to scroll down the screen and the moment was over.

"But back to the important subject—your safety." Meghan held up a hand. "Patricio Rodriguez also specializes in disaster control, vehicle modification—I think that means he can jack a car—perception training, and the dynamics of terror. Ninth-degree black belt in hapkido and a thirddegree black belt in aikido. A social chameleon who can blend in with any group. Qualified for conspicuous or inconspicuous protection. Excellent health. Six-three, one hundred ninety-five. Awarded the Sword of the Samurai for excellence in his profession by the National Bodyguard Association."

"I'm not sure someone who specializes in deadly weapons and the psychology of fear is anything near hot," Sadie responded. "Scary, yes. Hot, not so sure." Although she had to admit, she felt a little safer just being in the same space with his résumé. It was pretty impressive.

Then again, maybe his refusal to see Meghan was a sign. Maybe if Sadie just begged Bobby for more time to make her own personal security arrangements, he'd forget all about it when she ultimately didn't come up with any. "Why don't we just go?" She sighed. "Maybe you and I can look into some of the others tomorrow—"

"I know what you're thinking." Meghan narrowed her green eyes, gave Sadie a shrewd look. "You're thinking that if we just drag this out long enough, Bobby will forget all about it and go away."

Shoot. "Weeelll...."

"Not gonna happen." Meghan shook her head emphatically. "You should have seen him when he heard about what happened to you today in the parking lot. Veins were bulging out of his forehead." She tapped her own forehead to illustrate. "It wasn't pretty."

Feeling suddenly tired, Sadie eyed the cards in Meghan's planner. If she had to go through with this, what she really wanted was someone discreet, and Patricio Rodriguez, with or without his scary résumé, had proven his discretion with Jack. The thought of going with someone else, someone whose relationship with the tabloids was unknown, was almost as terrifying as being caught alone again with Lovesick.

"Look," Meghan broke into her thoughts. "On paper, Rodriguez is amazing. Even against the other impressive bodyguards I've dug up, he's clearly the best." She shook her PDA in Sadie's direction. "I think we should bring out the big guns. It's time for the 'Do you know who I am?' speech."

"The what?" She was playing dumb, but she knew exactly what Meghan was talking about—and she *so* didn't want to go there.

"Come on." Meghan opened the mini-fridge at her feet and fished out a Diet Coke for herself, popping open the top and taking a quick slug. "Every VIP I've worked for has a 'Do you know who I am?' speech or variation thereof. Works like a charm almost every time."

Sadie sighed. "And when it doesn't?"

"Well, then it's just embarrassing." Meghan bit a pink-glossed lip. "But I bet you have a great one."

Sadie wasn't quite sure how she was supposed to take that. "You know," she said, "I have a reputation. I'm the nice actress. The one who takes direction well and doesn't insist that the crew avoid eye contact with her. I can't go in there and be all 'Do you know who I am?' I never do that."

Meghan gave her a skeptical look. "No way."

"Okay, there was this one time back in the nineties when I wanted to get into the Viper Room and the bouncers didn't recognize me."

"Did it work?"

Jeez, the woman was like that bulldog she'd read about in the news that had bit down on a tire and had stayed there for days, refusing to let go.

She must have displayed some flicker of worry, though, because Meghan crowed triumphantly. "Ah-ha! I knew it! You so totally have to do it!"

"I don't think so." Folding her arms

across her chest, Sadie gave Meghan a look that said the discussion was closed.

"I'll call the police about Lovesick," Meghan countered. "Too bad things always leak to the press when you do that, and those tabloid reporters are really good at embellishing stuff...."

"Remind me to fire you when I get back." With a sigh, Sadie opened her car door and stepped out, feeling the sweat beginning to form on her forehead as she left the limo's cool air-conditioned environment for the hot California sun.

"I can't believe I'm doing this," she muttered to herself as she strode up the baby-palm-flanked walk to the imposing building.

Rodriguez and Associates was on the fifth floor, two offices down from the stairwell, with a set of double doors made from the same black-tinted glass as the outside windows. Squaring her shoulders, Sadie gripped the handle of one door and pulled it open.

The front office was a long room with a set of tasteful steel-gray chairs and couches with plum accent pillows in one corner, presumably for waiting clients. A black bookshelf with stacks of security-related books and magazines stood in another corner next to a water cooler. Potted tropical plants were interspersed throughout the long room. Four doors dotted the far wall, and in the center was a heavy black granite desk in the shape of a half-circle. And behind that sat the pit bull, she presumed.

He didn't look so bad. Cute. Nonthreatening. He was probably in his mid-twenties, although his round, apple cheeks might make people mistake him for younger. He wore a plaid short-sleeved shirt over a white T-shirt, and his hair was gelled and flatironed into the spiky, messy look so popular now. The name plaque on his desktop said his name was Troy Rodriguez. When she approached, he looked up and smiled, a slight dimple in one of his apple cheeks bringing out a semi-maternal response in her.

"Hi, there. How may I help you?" he asked, cheerfully.

"Well." *I can't do this,* she thought. *I can't do-you-know-who-I-am this guy! He looks so sweet.* "I'm here to see Patricio Rodriguez, please."

He visibly brightened, sitting up a little straighter in his chair. "Ah! You must be—" he pulled up an appointment calendar on the computer before him "—Walter Finkelbaum." His friendly smile turned into one of amused tolerance. "Why, Mr. Finkelbaum. How you've changed."

Taking a deep breath, Sadie tried again. "Right. Well, I'm not Mr. Finkelbaum, so maybe I could just wait until Mr. Rodriguez has an opening in his schedule?" She glanced toward the gray and plum couches.

Troy tilted his head to the right. "I'm sorry, ma'am. Mr. Rodriguez is all booked for the day, and there's a wait list for his services. Would you like me to put you on it?"

"You don't think he could just work me in?" She tapped her French manicure on the granite counter, taking care to look friendly and non-divalike. "It's kind of an emergency."

"I'm sorry to hear that, ma'am," Troy said, using the same exact inflection as before. "But Mr. Rodriguez isn't interested in acquiring more clients at this time. Would you like me to put you on the wait list for his services?"

Now, she was starting to feel a little less maternal towards Troy. "I can't go into the particulars, but I really need someone discreet and good at his job, and Mr. Rodriguez is allegedly both. Do you think I could just talk to him for five minutes?"

Troy's head was still tilted at what looked like a precise seventy-degree angle, and his smile was starting to look a little like someone had Botoxed it in place. "I'm sorry, ma'am, but Mr. Rodriguez just returned from Ecuador this morning, and he won't be able to see any extra visitors today. Would you like me to put you on the wait list?"

That was it. She'd had it with the little pit bull. Smacking her hands against the granite desktop, she leaned forward into Troy's space. "Do you have any idea who I am?"

"Mr. Rodriguez has a lot of important clients, Ms. Locke, and he's not taking any more at this time. Would you like me to—?"

"No!" Swallowing a curse that would have destroyed her "nice actress" reputation, she took a moment to compose herself. Even though she'd initially been resistant to the idea, the thought of a reliable, discreet bodyguard standing between her and Lovesick had started to feel comforting. And she just didn't want to let go of what little comfort she could get nowadays. But talking to Troy was getting her nowhere. She ground out a "thank you" and spun around on her Steve Maddens toward the door. But just as she reached it, her eye caught a glimpse of the magazine rack—filled to the gills with periodicals like *Scuba Divemaster*, *Xtreme Skydiving* and *Mountaineering*. She did a 180 and walked back to Troy the Stepford secretary.

He looked up, tilted his head, and smiled. The boy must have practiced that in the mirror, like her raised eyebrow.

"Listen, Troy," she said, leaning conspiratorially over his desk.

"I don't take bribes, ma'am."

She straightened in mock horror. "I'd never offer one. But I just thought I'd mention that we're going to be filming the *Jungle Raider* season finale in Washington state with those experimental wing suits we showed in *Jungle Raider IV*. You know, the kind where you jump out of an airplane and just sort of spread your wings?" She spread her arms out to demonstrate. "No parachute until you're just about ready to land? Ours are a new design—they fly longer and faster than any on the market today."

Troy narrowed his eyes at her.

"So," she continued, letting her arms fall back to her sides. "If you could just tell your boss that I might be able to pull a few strings in case anyone in my employ wanted to try them out…" She paused meaningfully. "I'd appreciate it."

"Mr. Rodriguez isn't taking any more clients at this time, ma'am. Would you—?" He was interrupted by the buzz of the intercom function from the phone on his desk. "Excuse me, please." He picked up the receiver. "Yes? Yes, Patricio. Yes, but—

But, I— But— Sure. I'll do that." Troy gritted his teeth, though his expression hadn't changed, giving his smile a slightly maniacal look. "It appears that Mr. Rodriguez has an opening in his schedule after all."

She glanced around the room, searching unsuccessfully for security cameras. "Was he listening in on our conversation?"

"He listens to everything, ma'am."

She nodded, matching Troy's sage expression. "Of course."

Troy gestured to the last door at the far end of the office. "Would you like me to show you into his office?"

"I'll be fine." She almost felt sorry for him. After all, he'd displayed the same blend of courtesy and stonewalling she expected from her own people. "You know, you're a really good secretary, Troy."

"I prefer security attaché, ma'am."

It took all of her acting skill not to bust out laughing. "Of course. Thanks again." And with that, she was in.

Chapter Three

The office was all windows. At least, three sides of it were windows, but the view was dazzling—blue, blue sky and swaying palm trees, not to mention the lushness of a small park across the street. Rodriguez and Associates was on a prime piece of real estate, that was for sure.

Which meant that Patricio Rodriguez probably made good money from his business. Which meant he had a lot of satisfied clients. Which meant maybe things would be okay, that she would be better off with him on her side against Lovesick, rather than remaining alone. For the first time in weeks, Sadie felt hopeful, even almost safe.

And then Rodriguez turned around.

He looked the way she expected Lucifer had just before he fell—dark, dangerous, beautiful. Not that she didn't see a lot of beautiful people in her line of work, but there was something there, some blend of intelligence and fearlessness and confidence in his striking light brown eyes that just took her breath away. Or maybe it was just the thought of his "My hands are registered lethal weapons" résumé, coming back to haunt her.

His hair was a glossy black, gelled into a fashionably disheveled spiky look, framing those singular eyes and a pair of prominent cheekbones. She had no doubt that he'd shaved that morning, but a light five-o'clock shadow had already started to dust his jaw. He wore an expensive-looking dark gray tailored shirt with an equally expensive-looking black suit that her couture-trained eye told her was Armani. The faintest scar—a thin white line that just barely caught the light—followed the line of his left eyebrow. It probably would have looked a lot worse if it hadn't been in a location that masked it. She wondered how he'd gotten it. She wondered what he was thinking...especially of her.

"Sadie Locke," he said. Even his voice was amazing, low and soft and...man, she needed to stop. Right now. Because he had the look of someone who could read her very easily, and she doubted he would like what he read. Instant infatuation was never an attractive quality.

"Mr. Rodriguez." She kept her face impassive, crinkling her eyes slightly at the corners to convey that she was unmoved, but open to friendly conversation.

Cocking his head toward an empty chair, Rodriguez turned abruptly away from her and walked behind his desk. Surprised at his move, she dropped the hand that had been poised a few inches away from her hip, waiting for a handshake that hadn't come.

Gorgeous and rude. What a lovely combination.

She folded herself into the fabric and steel chair, crossing her ankles delicately beneath her so her calves were in a perfect diagonal line. Interview pose—attractive and guaranteed to keep the cameras from inadvertently going up her skirt.

He'd sat down shortly after she had and was now leaning back in his expensive leather office chair, which cradled his back and head like a throne. "So," he said without preamble. "You have a stalker."

The statement startled Sadie right out of Interview Pose, and she leaned forward, hands clenching the armrests of her chair. "How could you possibly know that?" Meghan had promised not to mention why they were in need of personal security until she was face-to-face with Patricio Rodriguez himself. And Sadie had threatened to dump a litter of Siamese kittens in Jack's trailer if he so much as breathed a word. Who was left? The security guards at Franklin Studios thought the incident in the parking lot was a one-time prank by a die-hard fan. So how could Rodriguez have heard already? And how long would it take the tabloids to figure it out as well?

"Informed guess." He steepled his long fingers under his chin, looking a little bored. "Famous actress, comes to my office herself with an air of frantic desperation about her. Usually equals stalker."

"Air of frantic desper—" Well, that was attractive. She felt her body slump into her chair. Dammit, dammit, dammit. Years and years of trying to build up her defenses, to keep herself from caring one bit whether a reviewer hated her work or a magazine wrote something nasty about her, and she still couldn't deal when a perfect stranger didn't seem to immediately like her. And Patricio Rodriguez seemed to really not like her. Damn her freaky stage mom for making her the needy, psychological mess she was. This was what competing in beauty pageants starting at age two did to a person. This was how a television show at age twelve compounded it.

Rising from her chair, Sadie picked up her lilac Prada purse, squeezing the soft leather with both hands as if it were a comforting stuffed animal. What a huge mistake it had been, letting Meghan talk her into coming in here. She swallowed the reflexive apology for disturbing him—women apologized too much in general, in her opinion, and she hadn't done anything wrong by seeking his services. She didn't need some sniper trained, bomb defusing, carjacking, I'm-a-deep-and-mysterious-guy bodyguard around, anyway. "Thank you for seeing me, Mr. Rodriguez."

But before she could turn away, Rodriguez had come around the side of his desk and was standing before her, all tousled hair and whiskey-colored eyes. "Tell me about him," he said.

She just blinked at him, part of her wanting to tell him where to go, and part of her still wanting him to like her. Stupid, stupid beauty pageants. Stupid screwed up life. If she hadn't been so deadly afraid of a psychiatrist selling her neuroses in gross, exacting detail to a magazine, she might have actually tried therapy as a way of curing her constant need for approval. But instead of telling Patricio Rodriguez all of that, she simply stared at him, knowing that her silence coupled with the pale blue of her eyes had a discomforting effect.

It worked, sort of. Rodriguez didn't even blink in the face of the "ice-blue stare of death," as Meghan called it, but he did break the silence first. "Look, if this guy is serious, you need help. I can get you that help."

"I can get help elsewhere," Sadie replied, starting to turn toward the door.

"It started with letters, didn't it?" he interjected.

She stopped, squeezed her purse. "Well, yeah, but—"

"Friendly at first, and then they turned into threats?"

Unreal. She'd been ready to leave, and now he was looking at her all concerned, with that slight note of sympathy in his voice, and she immediately felt comfortable. Protected. Safe. Oh, this guy was good. "How…?"

Sadie let the question trail off as Rodriguez motioned for her to sit on a nearby couch, upholstered in soft, Italian leather. She sat, and he followed. "Has he contacted you in other ways? Phone calls? Face-to-face meetings?"

"Both."

Rodriguez's wide mouth twisted, the intensity in his expression telling her he didn't like that answer. "I assume because of who you are that your people make it hard to get close to you. If he's accessing your phone number and setting up meetings, he's serious. Start from the beginning, and tell me everything, even if it seems insignificant."

She tried to check herself, but details about Lovesick's behavior came pouring out of her. It felt good to tell someone about all of it, and Rodriguez was an amazing listener. He looked you right in the eye, nodded at all the right moments, and just made her feel like everything she said was the center of his universe for that moment. It was almost seductive, having a man listen like that, even if she was going to pay him for it.

So she told him, all about how she'd gotten a few fan letters from a friendly but smitten individual who signed himself "Lovesick"; how the letters had started taking on a more sinister tone, with Lovesick acting like they were already lovers in real life instead of in his fantasies. Of how the prank phone calls had started, coming to her unlisted and carefully protected home and cell phone lines. Those had been more overtly threatening. Finally she described today's attack, which still took her breath away the more she thought about it.

And this man before her... So maybe he wasn't a paragon of politeness, but Jack said she could trust him, and that was worth its weight in gold. Right now, she would pay nearly anything to have someone trustworthy and strong by her side.

"So, Mr. Rodriguez," she continued, "you come highly recommended by people...by friends, and I'd like to hire you. It'd be great if you could start immediately, but if you need to make other arrangements..." She flipped a hand in the air, leaving the rest of the sentence open.

"Are you looking for conspicuous or inconspicuous protection?" When she didn't reply, he explained. "Conspicuous protection is what the Secret Service provide the president. The suits and dark glasses tell everyone that the country's best security operatives are surrounding this person, and you'll have to get through them to get to him. Their presence is a deterrent to attacks. Inconspicuous protection is where your bodyguard blends in with the scenery, and no one is aware you've even hired protection. We blend into the social scene around us, maybe under the pretense of being your chauffeur or—" he looked down at his hand, toying with the pencil that he'd pulled out of his shirt pocket "—boyfriend. Well-known personalities like yourself sometimes choose this option if they want to keep their reasons for hiring a security specialist private. In other words, you don't get the deterrent of having obvious security around you, but you get a higher degree of discretion. As you can probably guess, my associates and I highly recommend conspicuous protection."

Sadie studied her French manicure. "I'd be tempted to go with inconspicuous, though. This guy isn't going to give up because he sees a man in designer sunglasses at my side. And I'd rather keep this whole thing from the press."

Rodriguez was silent for a moment, then

took a silver business card holder out of the inside pocket of his suit jacket, flipped it open, and held the top two out to her. "I have a couple of associates who specialize in stalking cases. I'll have them call you as soon as possible, but here's their contact info, just in case."

The thought of doing this all over again with another person threw her into abject panic. "But—"

He actually looked apologetic, damn the man. "You met Troy," he said. "Like the boy said, my workload is full."

She glanced at the cards in her hand. Floyd Thompson and Ben Olivera. Oh, no. No no no no no. She had no references for Floyd and Ben. Floyd and Ben hadn't been privy to Jack's most private neuroses and had kept quiet about them. Floyd and Ben weren't in Meghan's ever-reliable planner. If she couldn't have Patricio Rodriguez, she'd rather have no one, but no one wasn't an option right now. Now that Meghan had introduced the idea of someone who could protect her, from Lovesick and from the press, she was having a hard time letting that idea go.

"I'm sure they're great," Sadie began, "but I don't want anyone else. I heard you're the best, and…" She let her words trail off, and her vision blurred, a single warm tear spilling down her cheek. "The thing is, I'm scared to death. This guy, he's getting more and more violent, and I want to know when I step out of my house that I'm safe." She purposefully widened her tear-filled eyes and looked right at Rodriguez. "He has my car keys, and he hurt me today. And I'm so scared that he's going to—" She gasped and covered her mouth with a closed fist.

"Ms. Locke?"

She opened her eyes even wider until she felt like they were about to pop out of their sockets.

"Didn't you do that crying-speech-knuckle-to-the-mouth thing in your last film?"

"Mmm?" she said in reply around her clenched hand, shocked into silence.

"That scene where you're kidnapped and

threatened by Guatemalan rebels and you try to talk your way out of it?" he continued.

This was not her day. She let the hand at her mouth drop into her lap with a quiet thud.

"You had the rebel leader wrapped around your finger with that one. And then you kicked his ass."

Sadie supposed she should have been glad Rodriguez at least watched her movies, but it was little comfort in the face of her now-monumental embarrassment. Served her right for flying in the face of over a hundred years of feminism by trying to manipulate a man with tears. Desperation was a bad, bad thing.

She swiped at her long bangs with one hand, staring quietly out the window at the street below. "Well," she said quietly. "It was worth a shot." She picked up her purse once more and twisted the strap around her wrist. "I'm sorry to have bothered you. I just thought— Jack Donohue told me exactly how trustworthy you were when you worked for him, and I thought that maybe,

I could trust you, too." She forced the corners of her mouth to turn up in a polite smile, but that was all she had the energy to put into her polite façade. She was sure that she looked every bit as disappointed as she felt, but she didn't care. "Integrity like that is rare in this city, Mr. Rodriguez. I guess I just felt I needed someone like that around. Especially n—" She cut herself off with a brisk shake of her head. "Thank you. I'll tell Troy I'd be happy to be put on your waiting list."

He said nothing, simply held out the two business cards of his colleagues. She took them, then pushed herself off the couch and silently walked toward the door.

PATRICIO WATCHED her go, and though he was tempted, he didn't stop her. The door closed with a soft click, and then he was left in the nearmonastic silence of his office.

Shucking his suit jacket, he tossed it onto the couch and moved to sit behind his desk. Opening one of the filing cabinet drawers, he took out a bottle of scotch and a squat cut crystal glass, pouring until the glass was halfway full.

Then, he just stared at the warm, brown liquid. He wanted to pour it down his throat more than anything in the world at that moment. But just one drink, and he'd be back in oblivion again. And that was a place Patricio never wanted to return to.

He did this every once in awhile, tested himself, just to make sure he still had what it took to say no. For twelve years now, he'd always had. But he still wondered if a day would come....

Spinning around abruptly in his chair, he looked out the window at the park below, and his thoughts turned back to the woman who'd just come into his office and his life. Sadie Locke hadn't been anything like he'd expected. He'd seen her before— though she hadn't noticed him, he'd made sure of it—when he'd provided personal security for her co-star, Jack Donohue. So he knew she was good-looking, but talking with her was something else entirely. Not many of Hollywood's A-list came to his office themselves. They usually sent their lackeys or an obscenely expensive car to bring him to them. At least, on their first attempt.

Plus, the flight suit thing had been impressive—she'd either done her research on him or she was observant. And she'd held her own with his cousin Troy.

He'd expected an expensive-looking, fragile prima donna—with some healthy neuroses since she was friends with Jack Donohue. But instead, in her white halter and light purple skirt that fluttered around slender yet muscular thighs, she looked...strong. Fresh-faced and healthy.

Beautiful.

He scrubbed a hand across his face. God, he did not want to go there.

He wondered how long it would take to erase her image from his mind—the look of exasperation he'd seen on her pretty face throughout her visit, her habit of running an impatient hand through her short dark hair. That hair, which had probably been simply brown when she was younger, was streaked with a color like caramel apples and came to a point at the nape of her slender, graceful neck. He had a feeling he'd be thinking about the back of Sadie Locke's neck for a long time.

Feeling suddenly restless, Patricio pushed out of his chair and leaned a forearm against the window, letting his forehead rest on it. Directly below, he saw a Silver Shadow limo pull out of the front driveway, and Sadie Locke pull out of his life for good. It was better that way.

He wasn't good at anything personal, and things had immediately felt personal with Sadie Locke—ever since he'd overheard her conversation with Troy. She had the lamest "Do you know who I am" speech he'd ever heard. She was smart. She was kind. Give him a few days, and he'd be too close for his own comfort. A smoky bar and a one-night stand were usually enough to soothe his loneliness, and he wasn't about to put himself face-to-face with the alternative every damn day until her stalker was caught. From the minute she'd entered his office, he'd been hell-bent on one set of actions—give her the cards, give her assurances, get her out of there. And thank God it had worked.

He wondered how many people knew Sadie Locke had freckles on her nose.

Well, where the hell had that thought come from? Maybe he was overtired and overworked. Maybe he was freaking possessed.

He couldn't stop thinking about the back of her neck, her ice-blue eyes, the fear in them. Fear he could've helped banish, if he'd been half the man to get it done.

Fact was, he'd liked Sadie Locke. And he knew from experience that that would never end well. Not when she found out who and what he really was.

A FEW HOURS LATER, toward the end of his workday, Patricio saw his brother Joe's new Honda S2000 screech into a spot in the lot at the front of the building. Joe got out, followed by Patricio's twin brother, Daniel. He hadn't seen them since he'd gotten back from his last job protecting a millionaire software developer during a business trip to Ecuador. But he'd talked to them on the phone, so his pulse quickened at the thought of the news they'd bring with them.

Over twenty years ago, their parents had been murdered over a blackmail scheme gone bad—the blackmailer in question being their father, Ramon Lopez. Orphaned and with no extended family capable of taking them in, the brothers and their baby sister Sabrina had been immediately put up for adoption. While Patricio and his twin brother, Daniel, had been placed with one couple, Edgardo and Felicia Rodriguez, Sabrina and Joe had ended up in other situations. Having witnessed his mother's murder, Joe had had such severe emotional issues, he'd ended up in a foster home for troubled boys near San Francisco.

They had no idea what had happened to Sabrina.

Patricio and Daniel had tried for years to find Joe and Sabrina, but they kept running into dead ends, starting with the long-ago fire that had burned down the social services building where their records had been kept. But about a year earlier, they'd finally found Joe. And now, the three brothers were using every contact and resource they had to find their baby sister.

She'd been just eighteen months old when their parents had died. A chubby, happy baby who Patricio remembered with a clarity that seemed surprising since he'd only been five years old at the time. But he did remember her—her dimpled knees and Michelin Tire Man arms and legs, her dark, silken hair and sweet baby smell. He remembered the first time his mother had let him hold her, and how he'd felt so grown-up and responsible then, so protective of the little creature who sat on his small lap.

God, he hoped they'd found her this time.

Patricio walked to his desk, leaning against the front of it and hovering over the intercom buzzer. When it finally sounded, he immediately told Troy to send his brothers in. One look at their faces, and he knew.

"No joy, huh?" he said with a casualness he wasn't even close to feeling.

Joe threw himself into one of the chairs in front of his desk, frustration and disgust written all over his face. "Right age, right hair color, right birth date, wrong person," Joe said. "She'd already traced her biological parents, and they weren't the same as ours."

Daniel shut the door and walked directly to Patricio's desk, zeroing in immediately on the glass of scotch sitting on his desk. He picked up the tumbler, worry lines crossing his forehead. "Rico?"

Patricio grabbed it back. "Just a stupid ritual. Nothing to worry about, Mother. I never drink it." He made to dump it in a nearby potted rubber plant, embarrassed by his failure to hide the damned thing before his brothers had walked in. But Joe leaned forward, swiping at the glass as Patricio carried it past him. "Whoa, whoa, whoa. Gimme that." Patricio handed him the tumbler, and he drained it. "Thanks."

Danny glared at Joe. "Nice."

"What?" Joe shrugged, then crossed his arms defensively. "Wouldn't want it to go to waste. I believe Patricio when he says he wouldn't have touched it."

"You didn't see him when he would have," Danny muttered under his breath.

"What are you guys doing here?" Patricio asked, determined to change the subject. He beat himself up enough about his past—he didn't need to hear it from Danny, too. "You could have called and told me it was a dead end."

Joe slid the now-empty glass across Patricio's desktop, then sat back in his chair again. With a sigh, he looked up at the twins, leaning side by side against the desk. "See, we were thinking...."

"Uh-oh."

"Funny, Rico. Funnnnyyyy." Joe leaned forward, his elbows on his knees. "We need to visit Amelia Allen."

The words were like a hit to the solar plexus. "Are you high?" Patricio asked, emotion giving more snap to the words than he'd intended.

Joe gave him a crooked smile that didn't quite hit his eyes. "Noooo, but if you make me go by myself, I might wish I were."

"What the hell, Joe?" Patricio pushed off the desk, pacing to the door and back. Knowing Danny, he'd probably start doing the same in a moment, and then the two of them could wear a path in the carpeting. Despite the casualness with which Joe had brought her up, Amelia Allen wasn't a topic any of them liked to talk about.

Over twenty-five years ago, their father, Ramon Lopez, had discovered that the then-mayor of Los Angeles, a man who was now retired California Senator Wade Allen, had been having an affair. Though the brothers would never entirely know all of the motives behind Ramon's actions, they did know that greed had been a big one. He had started blackmailing Allen, extorting a substantial amount of money from the man. Unbeknownst to Allen, his wife Amelia found out about the scheme and had arranged to have Ramon murdered to save her husband's rising star. Then, believing that Ramon's wife Daniela was also involved, she'd had Daniela killed as well.

And the rest was the tragic history of the Lopez boys. The only witness to his mother's murder, Joe had coped with what he'd seen by wiping it completely from memory—along with the first ten years of his life. Daniel had become stoic, so adept at keeping in his emotions, it had nearly cost him the love of his life—and had kept them separated and at each other's throats for over a decade. And Patricio had just gotten angry, a deep, overwhelming anger at having his family ripped apart that had led him into the arms of one of Los Angeles's most brutal street gangs.

He wasn't proud of what he'd done—he'd spend the rest of his life atoning for what his time with the Latin Cobras had done to his adoptive parents, to his twin brother and to one innocent girl he'd watched die at the hands of his gangbanger "brothers," too wasted to stop her murder.

Sure, he'd made his own decisions, and he'd have to live with them, but his chain of bad choices had started when Amelia Allen had given the order to tear apart his family.

He hadn't met her—only Joe and Danny had gone to her trial and subsequent sentencing. They'd also tried to talk to her in prison, to find out what she might know about Sabrina, but Amelia had stubbornly refused to say a word, beyond a few pleasantries.

As for Patricio, he didn't want to meet her. Gang life had left him with a series of addictions—to alcohol, to violence, to numbing even the most insignificant pain he felt the easiest way possible. He'd managed to finally free himself from all of them, but he was afraid that if he saw Amelia Allen, he'd want to kill her. And if he let himself feel that kind of violence again, his carefully repaired life would crumble back into the state of chaos he'd worked so hard to crawl out of.

"When?" Patricio asked. "And, more importantly, why?"

"Day after tomorrow. Only day I could get off work," Danny said, darting a glance at Joe, who took his cue.

"Just before she was arrested for our parents' murders, Amelia told me she'd 'arranged for good homes for all you Lopez children,'" Joe reminded him. "So, there's a good chance she knows who adopted Sabrina or, at least, which agency handled the adoption. And we're not going to stop asking until she tells us what we need to know."

Patricio gave a low whistle, again, displaying a casual attitude to mask the emotions inside.

"You don't have to go, Rico," Joe told him, making it clear he didn't buy the act. "Seriously."

Patricio took a deep breath, and then, suddenly, detached. His pulse slowed, his gut stopped churning, and he felt like his insides had been coated with a sheet of ice. Ice that allowed him to go through the motions without feeling anything. Ice that allowed him to breathe. The ability had served him well in his gangbanger days, let him jack cars, get into fights, damage property with no fear.

"No," he said. "I'll go. I should have gone before. If Amelia Allen knows where Sabrina is, I want to be there when we get it out of her."

Chapter Four

The next day, Patricio pulled his black Pontiac GT in the parking lot of the Southern California Women's Facility, a medium-security prison in Los Angeles where Amelia Allen would spend the next thirty-plus years of her life. He saw Joe and Daniel waiting for him near the prison's visitor entrance.

Go time.

Tugging his cell phone out of his pocket, he flipped it open. Troy answered on the second ring.

"Did she call yet?" Patricio asked.

"No, sir," Troy said, knowing exactly who the "she" in question was. "I can call you immediately if she does."

Damn. Thanking Troy, he snapped the

phone shut. Over twenty-four hours had gone by since Sadie Locke's visit, and she still hadn't returned the phone calls of the two security specialists he'd referred. Which meant she was out there alone while her stalker waited for another opportunity to get close to her. And since, like most human beings, she was probably sticking to her usual routines and behaviors, it would only be a matter of time before that happened. From the way she'd described the guy's escalating behavior, it was obvious the situation was serious.

She came to you for help. And what did you do?

Smacking his hand against the steering wheel, Patricio pushed all thoughts of Sadie Locke out of his head as he shoved his phone in the pocket of his jeans. Slamming the car door behind him, he headed for where his brothers were waiting at the prison entrance. After the usual security checks, they were led inside by a couple of guards to the room where inmates received visitors. Since it was only a medium-security prison, they'd have an hour of face-to-face conversation with Amelia Allen at a small table, no Plexiglas required.

One of the guards motioned them inside a room where several women in jeans and light blue button-down shirts were seated, waiting for their visitors to arrive. It only took a moment for the brothers to spot the former senator's wife, her once-blond hair now shot with gray and her pale, lined face devoid of makeup. Her hair was pulled back in a ponytail instead of the French twist they'd grown accustomed to seeing on television.

She rose as they approached the table. "Well…hello," she greeted them in her soft voice, her Alabama roots still evident in her accent. "I've been sitting here thinking of what I'd say to you boys, and I swear, I just don't know…."

The three of them simply stared at her. Patricio couldn't believe that this tiny, polite woman had actually hired a hitman to kill their parents. All to save her husband's political career and keep her own place as a powerful politician's wife.

It was pathetic. She was pathetic.

Amelia's hands fluttered around her ponytail for a moment, but then she sat on one of the plastic and metal chairs surrounding the round formica table. "Won't you sit?" she asked them.

Danny and Joe sat. Patricio remained standing.

"Mrs. Allen," Joe began.

Her thin mouth twisted as she studied Patricio. "You must be the other twin, the one who got involved with those gangs."

Her words shouldn't have stung, but they did. To some people, Patricio would always be the one who'd been in a street gang. But for God's sake, the woman was a murderer. Who was she to judge him? Who was she to look at him like that, to condemn his bad choices?

Then again, some had called him a murderer, too.

"We have a couple of questions we'd like to ask you," Joe said, keeping his voice calm and well-modulated, as if he were talking to a child.

Amelia narrowed her eyes, tilting her head to the side as she eyed Joe suspiciously. "What on earth could you possibly have to ask me?" Patricio noticed that her nails were bitten to the quick. At least prison life wasn't agreeing with her—they had that consolation.

"It's about our sister, Sabrina," Danny interjected. "As we mentioned last time we saw you, she was about eighteen months old."

When our parents died, Patricio mentally finished his brother's sentence. He couldn't believe the stoic calm of his twin's voice, though he of all people knew best how Danny dealt with stress of any kind. But the man acted as if they were discussing the freaking weather.

Patricio's head pounded from the brightness of the dusty fluorescent lights hanging above, from the grating sound of Amelia Allen's voice. He wanted to punch something, break something, just to make himself feel better.

"Oh, yes. The little baby." Amelia nodded, her expression still wary.

"Mrs. Allen, you told me you'd found homes for all of us in the Lopez family,"

Joe said. Damn, he sounded like they'd been a charity project of Amelia's, not victims of her twisted ambition. "We've been trying to find her, and we haven't had any luck. We—"

"Want to know if I can help you?" she asked, her mouth turning upwards in a small smile. "Give you a lead? This is your third visit. I know the routine."

Resting her chin on her hand, she pondered the men before her for a few seconds while they simply waited. Then, some of her former sparkle came back into her blue eyes as she said, "I don't think so."

"You can't help us?" Danny asked. "Or, you won't?"

She glanced up at the ceiling. "Can't, won't, what does it matter?"

Patricio's hands had clenched so hard into fists, his short nails were digging into the skin of his palms. How could she do this, taunt them like this, after what she'd done? He moved between where his brothers sat, put his palms flat on the table. "Amelia," he said. Something in his voice, in his face, made the woman shrink back, her eyes wide as she clutched the edge of the table. "You might think the guards and walls of this prison will protect you, and they will, but not from me."

"Jesus, Rico," Danny whispered beside him. Patricio barely heard his brother, feeling like the ice inside him had encased his whole being. He leaned toward Amelia.

"I promise you," he said, his voice low, "if you don't tell us what you did with our sister, I will bury you. In the most painful way possible."

"Patricio Joaquin, *que dices?*" Joe asked him. *What are you saying?*

"Are you threatening me?" Amelia placed a palm on her upper chest.

Patricio didn't respond.

"Your threats mean nothing to me," she said, her voice rising with every word. "Your dirty, no-good father would have ruined my husband's career with his blackmailed threats, and you are just like him."

For about two seconds, Patricio remained quiet, and then with a suddenness that startled everyone in the room, he slammed his hand hard against the table.

The impact made the table rattle loudly, and his brothers jumped back in alarm.

"Where," he ground out, "is my sister?"

Joe and Daniel rose to stand behind him, but instead of rebuking him as he'd half expected, they simply stayed put, in silent support of his question.

He felt arms grabbing him on either side, heard shouting from somewhere far away. "Where is she?" he hissed, and then the ice started slipping away, and all he could do was feel. His head pounded, and his eyes started to sting.

Amelia Allen didn't say a word as the guards led him away.

TWO DAYS WENT by, and fortunately, the man Sadie knew only as Lovesick didn't make an appearance. Maybe he'd followed her to Rodriguez and Associates. Maybe the mere act of searching for a personal security specialist had made him decide he was in over his head.

Something told her she was deluding herself, but she didn't care. She drove to and from work alone, lived alone in a Beverly Hills mansion, spent most of her free time alone. If it took a little delusional thinking to keep her from freaking out, then that's what she'd do.

As she entered her house after driving herself—alone—from work, she kicked off her shoes, leaving them by the door. Immediately heading upstairs, Sadie changed into a fitted T-shirt and a pair of cotton pajama bottoms with the words "drama queen" printed all over them, which had been lying on top of the wicker clothes hamper inside her bedroom-size walk-in closet. She left her jeans and white button-down shirt in their place in a crumpled heap. She could pick them up tomorrow—right now, she just wanted to crawl into bed. Bobby had been particularly brutal today, making them shoot and reshoot the same scene over and over again. Not to mention that Jack kept busting out laughing at random moments, the goober.

After a trip to the kitchen to make a quick cup of sleep-inducing chamomile tea, Sadie sank into the soft white sheets of her bed. Her home was decorated to look like a villa in Tuscany, all rich fabrics, stuccoed walls, Italian antiques and artwork, and her bedroom was a soothing lavender, white and Wedgwood-blue oasis in the heart of it. Her tea steaming on the nightstand next to her, she pulled a book off the small stack on her nightstand, hoping it would be as good as the blurb on the dust jacket promised. As she cracked open the spine of her book, she caught a movement out of the corner of her eye.

A shadow crept slowly across the wall. Someone was outside her window.

Sadie shot upright, dropping the book onto her puffy blue comforter. Her heart hammered inside her chest, and she could only watch as the shadow inched from one side of the wall to the other. At the last moment, a movement, like a head turning.

She prayed it was just her imagination, just her two security dogs roaming about the yard. But she knew it was no such thing. She'd had the dogs for a couple of years now, and she'd never seen anything like that.

It's not Lovesick. It's not Lovesick. But

the mantra she murmured under her breath did little to soothe her. Her hand went to her temple, which still felt tender to the touch.

So afraid of what she might see, Sadie kicked her legs free of the comforter and looked out through the paned glass window next to the head of her bed. She couldn't see much from her faraway angle, other than a few leaves of the night-blooming jasmine bush she'd had planted underneath it, and darkness beyond that. And then she sensed something out of the corner of her eye that had her spinning back around.

Another shadow. Another movement.

I know you love me. We're meant to be.

Such a big house. And she was all alone.

With one quick movement, Sadie reached over and snapped off the brass Stieffel lamp on her nightstand, so she could take a better look out the window without revealing herself. Moonlight from the outside bathed the room in a bluish-gray glow. She sidled across the king-size mattress until her feet hit the edge of the bed, trying hard to be quiet, until she realized how ridiculous she was being. An intruder outside wasn't going to be listening for her—he'd be searching the outside of her house for an easy way in. Mentally running through potentially vulnerable spots in her home, she sank to the floor and carefully crept to the window.

All she saw was the large expanse of perfectly trimmed grass, tipped silver in the moonlight.

"Which is exactly what's supposed to be out there, you paranoid freak," she muttered to herself. Not only would an intruder have to scale the wall without being seen by her neighbors, but he'd have to get over the broken glass embedded on top of it, jump down without breaking any bones and *then* he'd have to disarm her household security system without triggering the automatic tamper alert, which would notify the nearest branch of the LAPD. She was perfectly safe. Even Jada Winthrop would have a hard time busting through that kind of security.

Then again, it couldn't hurt to call someone—Meghan, maybe, or Jack—just to let them know what was going on. Feeling across the top of her nightstand in the darkness for the phone, her hand connected with the cordless handset. She punched in Meghan's number, having no problem getting it right by feel.

Sadie hung up before her assistant's phone even had a chance to ring. The woman was her employee, and it seemed grossly unfair to bother her at ten-thirty at night over a case of the heebies when Meghan was officially off duty. Besides, if anyone did try to get inside Sadie's house, her silent alarm system would automatically dial 911 and electronically let the authorities know she needed help. Dropping the phone into its cradle, she picked up her nearly empty tea mug, hugging it to her chest for comfort, though it made a poor weapon. And she waited.

Minutes ticked by, and no more shadows floated across her window to terrorize her, no strange noises came from the farthest regions of her home. She was fine. Everything was fine.

Creak.

There was only one loose board in her house that made that noise, and it was mere feet from her bedroom door.

Which had no locks.

Someone was in her house.

She glanced at the window, wondering if she could survive a jump through it, two stories down. And then, still clutching the mug in one hand, she burst through the door, running for her life. She barreled down the hallway, grabbing the banister at the top of the stairs and swinging around it, hurling herself down the steps.

About halfway down, the security keypad near the front door came into view.

It was off.

She made it to the bottom of the stairs, taking the last four at a single jump that made the soles of her bare feet sting. She lunged for the keypad. Smacking her palms against the wall near the keypad, Sadie halted her forward momentum and started punching buttons, trying to activate the alarm. The red light blinked once, but the system didn't respond. Glancing upstairs behind her, she could only see darkness, could only hear her heart hammering in her ears. She tried again.

Nothing.

She heard the faintest noise upstairs, like a soft footfall on the wood floors.

Oh, no. She entered the code once more. It still didn't respond. She started for the front door.

He could see her.

Sadie immediately doubled back, heading instead for the kitchen and the patio doors that would take her closer to the side gate, where she could escape, could perhaps get to one of her neighbors for help without being seen. If she went through the front door, he'd know exactly where she'd gone.

Slowing slightly to keep her bare feet from making a smacking sound on the marble tiles, Sadie moved quickly silently into the kitchen. As she passed the counter, her hand closed around the handle of one of the knives in her nearby butcher block. She pulled it out, the metal singing softly when it moved against the wood. She kept her eyes on the patio doors just ahead, watching the soothing motion of the chiffon curtains flanking them wafting upward in the breeze.

Oh, God.

The curtains.

Her pulse quickened into triple time as panic coiled around her chest. Because what she'd seen told her she'd made a very big miscalculation.

Clutching the knife to her chest, she remained completely still, watching the floating curtains, feeling a breeze that she shouldn't have been feeling since she never left those patio doors open. But that wasn't what held her frozen in sheer terror.

A figure stood just inside, motionless in the darkest area near the dining room corner. The curtains floated upward again, obscuring him from her vision for a split second before the breeze died once more. She had no idea how long he'd been standing there, watching her, waiting for her.

Lovesick.

I'll make you remember you love me.

Her breath catching in revulsion at the mental echo of his words, Sadie gripped the knife, wondering if it would protect her, wondering if she'd last the night. He'd gotten past her alarm system, so there would be no police on their way, unless she managed to keep away from him somehow, managed to get to a phone.

He moved, just the slightest turn of his head.

Now!

Sliding the knife in her hand so she held it by the blade, Sadie did the only thing she could.

She threw it with all her strength at his head.

The shadow ducked, and the knife embedded itself in her wall with a thunk, directly behind where the man's head had been.

"Locke! Christ!" Patricio Rodriguez stepped into view.

Sadie jumped at his words, but then her body relaxed as she recognized his face as he stepped into the light of her kitchen. A nasty, clammy chill crept across her skin—

the kind you got after nearly missing an accident in your car or avoiding a dangerous fall—and then it was gone, taking the last of her terror with it, leaving only relief.

Wait a minute. Rodriguez had refused to let her hire him, and now he'd broken into her house, despite the fact that no normal person should have been able to do that. What the heck? Her skin prickled again, her pulse quickening. What if he was insane? What if he were here because he wanted to harm her? Shooting a quick glance at the phone, Sadie wondered if she could get to it and dial 911 before he—

"Don't be afraid," he said. And before she could react, he moved swiftly, pulling a cell phone from the side pocket of his cargo pants. And then he was beside her, pressing the phone into her hand, giving her a set of keys. "Call the police. My car is parked outside. Get in, and drive." And then he was running past her, heading for the stairs.

Barely able to think as she listened to the footsteps running above her upstairs, Sadie called the police, reporting a possible intruder as she headed for the front door.

She heard a shout and the sound of breaking glass, and then Patricio was running back down the stairs. He pulled open the front door, then stopped himself. Turning to look at her, he muttered a few Spanish phrases under his breath. She didn't remember much from her college Spanish classes, but she did know how to translate an f-bomb when she heard one.

"I told you to get out of the house, *mujer,*" he said, his face intense and angry as he stalked toward her. He was all in black—black cargo pants tucked into black military boots, black T-shirt, black stocking hat pulled over his hair. Even his face had black and green camouflage paint smeared all over it, making his unusual light-brown eyes stand out even more.

"I didn't have time," she responded, wondering why he was so angry, what had happened upstairs. "What was that?"

"What's the matter with you, Locke?" he continued. "What happened to 'I need to know I'm safe when I leave my house'? You're not even safe in it."

"I'll say it again," she said calmly, crossing her arms. "What happened upstairs?"

"Someone broke into your house. If I hadn't been outside…" He let his words trail off, and his expression lost its intensity, leaving only concern in its wake.

She couldn't even deal with the words he'd just spoken, with what had just happened. Her chest felt like someone was sitting on it, and she gulped oxygen like a dying woman. "You were—?" Outside. He'd been outside.

It was too much. The swirl of emotions inside her threatened to overwhelm her, so she pushed aside the true issue—the intruder—and seized on something less complicated—anger.

Silently she stalked forward and slammed the front door closed, snapping the locks. Then, she spun around and stalked into the kitchen, where she shoved the patio doors closed and locked them as well. Patricio followed.

Her eyes landed on the knife protruding from the wall, marring the pale terra cotta wash on the stucco. Gritting her teeth, she yanked it free, then moved to stand directly in front of Rodriguez, giving him the best view of the full sound and fury of her emotions. "How did you—?" she sputtered, too upset to get a decent grasp on the English language. "The wall." She gestured wildly with the knife toward her enclosed front yard. "The alarm." She glanced toward the front door, unable to completely process the number of security failures that had just occurred. "The gate. My locks." Her jaw worked furiously for a moment. "God!" She tossed her hands angrily in the air. "And *what* are you doing here, anyway?"

"Your security needs an upgrade," Rodriguez said, looking slightly baffled by her anger. She might have felt sorry for him if she'd actually *invited* him to come. But she hadn't, so she pushed aside her mild pity and simply glared at him.

Holding his palms up so they faced her, Rodriguez took two steps away from her, and she had to admit, the nonthreatening pose made her feel less like a trapped rabbit. He gestured at the phone with his chin.

"My associates left what they described as a, quote, 'buttload' of messages on your machine," he said. "You didn't call them, and you're in serious danger. As your visitor tonight should have demonstrated."

"You refused to take me on as a client, so, danger or no, I have no idea what you're doing going all Delta Force in my front yard." Sadie waved the knife in his direction, pointy side out. "So not only do I still not know what you're doing here, but I have an insane stalker breaking through my security, I have a hole in my wall and I don't need a lecture on top of it."

"You should put that away." He leaned against the wall, crossing his arms as if this were a casual conversation. "Knives are dangerous."

"Thank you," she said, unable to hold back the sarcasm. "No wonder you are the number one security expert to the stars." The knife was back up, jabbing the air. "Who do you think you are, James—" jab "—freaking" jab "—Bond?—" jab.

A corner of his wide mouth turned up in a half smile. He couldn't actually find this funny, could he? She was half-tempted to throw the knife again, and this time, she wouldn't miss.

"Actually, Helen Keller could have gotten through your security," he said. "Seriously."

Then, before she could comprehend what he was doing, Rodriguez came off the wall in a blur and scissored his arms into an X in front of him, palms out. The thumb sides of his hands chopped her knife hand between them, connecting at the back of her palm and just below her wrist. The quick impact made her wrist bend and her hand spring open involuntarily. And the knife went hurtling across her cherry wood floor.

"Ow!" she exclaimed, more from surprise than any pain.

"That didn't hurt," Rodriguez informed her.

She was about to tell him that hell yes, it hurt, and she was going to come after him with a team of lawyers so shrewd, he'd be lucky to keep his hair gel after the hundred lawsuits they slapped him with. But then he reached for her hand, cradling it in both of his, and everything just stopped—her anger, her fear, his mild amusement. Even time seemed to stop.

He was right, she realized from somewhere in her now-fuzzy mind, it hadn't hurt at all. She could only watch as he checked the skin on the back of her hand, then turned it gently over to examine her wrist.

"I wouldn't have done that if it would hurt you. You throw like an Amazon. I wasn't taking any chances," he said, a corner of his mouth tilting upward.

"Stunt coordinator showed me how," she murmured, somewhat mesmerized by his touch.

"I'm sorry I scared you," he said quietly, still holding her hand.

His actions shocked her into silence. No one touched her—at least not unless it was under the orders of a director. But the people who worked for and around her always kept a respectful distance. Even people seeking autographs or a moment to offer a compliment on *Jungle Raider* stayed out of her personal space, as if an invisible bubble existed around her that they would not breach. Her co-stars always asked her how she did that, since they were often the subject of random gropings from overeager fans in public. She hadn't dated in awhile, preferring being alone to being tabloid fodder. And she hadn't seen her parents in ages—not that she would have let them touch her if she had.

So when Patricio took her hand, even though it was obvious he was just inspecting it for damage or redness, it took her breath away.

You don't know him. And he doesn't even like you, she reminded herself. But she couldn't seem to pull away. He kept running his fingers along her skin, and all she could do was feel.

"Patricio," she murmured.

He went completely still, only his incredible, unreadable eyes moving upward to look her in the face. Light hit the scar above his eyebrow, obvious even under all that camouflage paint, and she noticed that it was more jagged and severe than she'd previously thought. He stared at her for a moment, and his expression changed, suddenly, to something entirely different from his customary one of dispassionate boredom. He was so close to her, and he looked....

He looked hungry. And heaven help her, she felt it, too.

Sirens sounded outside as the police pulled up in front of her gate. He dropped her hand. She backed away.

"Can I call you that?" she asked softly, her mind still half-muddled over whatever that was that had just happened between them. "Do you mind?"

He straightened, and the shuttered, bored look was back. "You can call me whatever you want. You're the boss."

She'd studied people, scrutinized enough expressions and emotions and reactions in her line of work to recognize that the shift hadn't been her imagination. There was more to the man than he wanted to reveal, and she'd have to be very, very careful about taking his actions and words at face value.

If he was going to keep popping up in her life, that is.

He turned away, moving toward the front door and the sirens. She followed him, hitting the release button for the security gate on the way.

"Thank you for stopping him," she said to his back. "You still haven't told me exactly why you're here, but that doesn't mean I'm not glad you showed up."

"Someone at your studio who works for Bobby Hayes called us. Made us an offer we couldn't refuse." He opened the front door and turned around to face her. "So until your stalker is caught, you and I are going to be seeing a lot of each other."

Patricio Rodriguez, in her space, 24/7. Oh, my.

Then again, Sadie reminded herself, his motive for being here obviously had nothing to do with her. He hadn't wanted her money. He hadn't cared about her safety or comfort. He hadn't even flinched when she'd cried. But somehow, Bobby's people had thrown around enough of their money or influence or both for him to change his mind and take her on as a client.

Well, at least she knew where she stood.

Chapter Five

"You should sleep." Patricio shut the door behind the two detectives who had responded to Sadie's call. He nodded at her pajamas in a way that was thoroughly polite and professional, not commenting at all on the fact that they had "drama queen" stamped all over them. "There are some things we need to go over, but we can do that in the morning."

She briefly wondered if his words were a more polite version of Bobby's, "Locke, you look tired." He seemed instantly comfortable with this whole bodyguard thing, while she still felt slightly off-kilter at the arrangement. Not that she wasn't glad to have him around, especially with the gaping broken window in her spare bedroom

serving as a reminder of what had happened that night. The intruder had climbed
down a palm tree just outside the window,
which was how he'd eluded Patricio. Patricio might have caught him, but she
guessed that he hadn't been willing to take
a chance on leaving her alone.

She was glad.

Sadie started for the stairs, Rodriguez
walking companionably beside her. "I'll
make up a bed for you in the room down
the—"

"Don't bother."

She halted at the foot of the stairs, one
hand on the cherry wood banister, polished to a high sheen. "Where are you
going to sleep?"

"I'm not." He motioned for her to start
going up, which she did, craning her neck
to look at him as she walked.

"You're kidding, right?"

"No," he responded, coming up behind
her. "24/7 protection means you get protection 24/7."

They reached her bedroom door and she

rested one hand on the doorjamb, turning to face him. "So you won't sleep?"

"No. Tomorrow night, I'll have one of my associates stay outside your bedroom door while I sleep. But tonight, I'll be right here." He gestured to the space immediately outside her bedroom door. "Keeping watch."

She blinked at him, not knowing what to say. It seemed like too much effort, too much inconvenience for a small-town Minnesota girl. But then again, she supposed Franklin Studios was paying him well to ensure that the lead actress in one of their most lucrative shows remained safe. So she just went inside her bedroom and pushed a small-yet-comfortable, stuffed armchair into the hallway for him.

As soon as he saw what she was doing, Rodriguez took the chair from her, picking it up effortlessly and placing it so it directly faced her door. "Thanks." He sat down, combat-boots planted firmly on the floor, one arm on each of the armrests. The chair was rather feminine—upholstered in white with delicately etched blue flowers, but he didn't seem to mind. It made quite a picture, the guy who looked like he'd stepped out of *Apocalypse Now* sitting in such a frilly piece of furniture.

Her bangs fell across one eye, and she pushed them back, wondering briefly what kind of state her hair was in. Then again, he'd seen her drama queen pajamas, so her hair probably didn't matter. "Can I get you something to drink?"

"No, thanks," he replied. He pulled off his hat and shoved it in one of his side pockets, scrubbing his hands through his black hair until it once more looked artfully tousled instead of plastered to his skull. Which was so totally unfair—her hair was short, but if she'd been wearing a stocking cap, she'd have major hat head no matter how much she tried to fluff it back up.

"A magazine?" she offered. "Radio?"

"Nope."

Man, she'd be so bored in his place. Sitting there in her delicate chintz armchair in his military gear, he definitely looked out of place and…underutilized. "Do you want to wash your face?"

"Later."

Oookay, then. "Good night, Patricio."

"Night, Ms. Locke."

"It's Sadie, not Ms. Locke." She'd started to close her door, but then stopped at his words. "And thank you. So much." Despite the earlier scare, she really did feel grateful. For the first time in months, she might actually get some sleep, instead of jumping at every noise and shadow inside and out of her giant house.

He didn't respond, which made her nervous. And when she was nervous, her mouth tended to go into overdrive without her. That moment was no exception, and she found herself blurting out the thought that had been in her head since he'd made it clear where he'd be spending the night. "Is it lonely? Watching over people in the dark like this, just observing their lives with no one to keep you company? I don't know how you do it." Immediately she wished she could take it back, especially when she saw the brief scowl on Rodriguez's face.

"It's my choice." He stood, putting one hand on the edge of the door as if he were about to shove her inside and hold it closed. "Keep this in mind, *Ms*. Locke," he said, his face close to hers and his tone all business. She could smell the grease in his facepaint, see the five-o'clock shadow poking through the black and green smudges on his chin. "We're not friends. I'm not doing you a favor by being here. I'm being paid well to protect you, and believe me, I will keep you safe. In return, you will listen to everything I tell you, and you will follow my orders without question. You will not speak to me in public unless it's absolutely necessary, and you will get yourself used to acting like I'm not even there most of the time when I'm with you. I will protect you. But I will not be your friend or your confessor, and my personal business is my own. Are we clear?"

She couldn't speak, could barely breathe. In fact, it took all of her inner reserves just to keep meeting his hard-edged gaze. It hurt, having him talk to her like that, like she was just a bag of money to watch over and periodically extract funds from. Like he hated her so much, he wanted nothing more than for them to act like the other didn't exist when they were together.

But then, something flickered in his light brown eyes. Something vulnerable, and maybe even a little bit lost. It was a look she recognized, because it mirrored how she often felt.

She'd instinctively backed away while he was talking, but now that he'd stopped, she stepped forward, until she was in his space. He was taller than she was, and she had to crane her neck slightly to keep his gaze. But in her profession, she'd learned early on how to make someone give you his full attention, and Rodriguez was doing just that.

"What did someone do to you, Patricio?" she asked softly. She was blurting again, but she didn't care, wanted to get to him just like he'd gotten to her. "Who made you so angry? How did they get you to push everyone away as soon as you meet them?" If that wasn't the pot calling the kettle a people pusher, she didn't know what was, but her own neuroses weren't the issue at the moment.

He simply stared at her, his expression

unreadable. Several seconds ticked by, with them looking into each other's eyes, silent. He looked bored and slightly annoyed—again—but she knew she'd seen something else there. And some perverse impulse inside her didn't want to let that go. Most Hollywood bigwigs probably would have fired him after a speech like that, which meant that to achieve the kind of success he had, he didn't give that speech all too often. She was dying to know what it was that made her so special.

He was the first one to break the silence. "Good night, Ms. Locke," he said. The finality of his tone told her he considered the conversation over. All right, then. Over it would be. At least, for now.

He backed away, and she started to close the door. Then, another thought had her opening it again. He was seated, so she had the advantage this time, able to look down on him for once.

"Patricio, I'm fine with the boundaries you're setting. Follow orders, no questions, no complaints, no warm fuzzies. Lovesick means business, and if I have to have a bodyguard, I'm glad it's you, and I want to keep you happy. But I have one request," she said. "As your new employer."

He sat back in his chair and raised his dark eyebrows. How could the man look so darn bored all the time?

"Call me Sadie. Or I will make any divas you've worked with seem like a troupe of Girl Scouts. Including Jack Donohue." With that, she entered her bedroom and closed the door behind her.

PATRICIO SPENT the night thinking about the curve of Sadie Locke's neck, about her Amazon attitude in the face of what had to be a frightening situation.

It wasn't at all what he'd wanted to concentrate on while he kept himself awake and alert, but images of her and her Audrey-Hepburn-style grace kept popping into his head when he'd least expected it, least wanted it. And after six hours of staring at her closed bedroom door, knowing she was behind it, in her bed, trusting him to keep her safe, he'd had more thoughts of her than he cared to admit.

He wasn't sure what had made him snap like that, had made him give her that "we are not friends" speech, but he wasn't proud of himself. Not only had it been unprofessional, but it hadn't been necessary. In his line of work—and long before he'd gotten started in it, truth be told—he'd learned to master those nonverbal cues that made people keep their distance. And it worked, on the job and off. In a business where it was normal to have clients get attached to you, most of his had no such issues. But something about Sadie Locke just kept him off balance.

He didn't like it.

Scrubbing both hands through his hair, Patricio shifted in the frilly chair she'd brought out for him. *Don't think about her. Don't think about her. At least, not in the way that you're thinking about her, you unprofessional hack.*

But the internal command had the opposite effect, and suddenly her pale blue eyes and soft skin popped into his head like that damn Martian from the Flintstones cartoons he and his brother Daniel had watched as kids. But Sadie Locke was no cartoon Martian. Despite the short, funky haircut, she reminded him of a star from the forties. She was old-school pretty. She was dangerous.

Dangerous enough that he hadn't been able to just leave it alone after he'd refused her request for help. When twenty-four hours had passed and she hadn't returned any of the calls from the associates whose business cards he'd given her, Patricio had taken matters into his own hands. He knew Don and Marilyn Franklin—the brother-sister team who'd built *Jungle Raider*'s Franklin Studios from the ground up—having helped them train the security personnel who kept watch over the grounds. Worried that Sadie might have backed out of seeking personal protection altogether—when it was evident her stalker meant business—he'd called Marilyn. Marilyn, in turn, had gone to see Bobby Hayes, and the rest was history. They hadn't made him any offer other than to follow his standard payment schedule.

But Sadie didn't need to know that.

He simply hadn't been able to let it rest until he'd made sure Sadie Locke had the protection she'd been seeking. And since she and her bosses had made it clear she'd only take it from him, he had no choice but to provide it.

Stupid nagging conscience. Wasn't his fault if she wouldn't accept the services of any of his eminently qualified associates. But noooo. He just couldn't let it go. As soon as he'd invited her to tell him the gritty details of her unwanted relationship with the stalker, he'd reached the point of no return with Sadie Locke.

A FEW HOURS LATER, as the warm California sunshine began to filter through the gigantic house, Patricio could hear Sadie moving around behind the door. He stood, stretched his arms above his head and then sat back down again. She'd be coming out soon, and he didn't feel ready for it, for her.

He heard a muffled scream come from inside her room. Without even stopping to think, he shot up from the chair and burst through the door. Sadie was standing in the doorway to her bathroom, one arm wrapped tightly across her stomach, her other hand covering her mouth. She was looking at something inside the room. He stepped forward to see.

Someone had written "Who is he?" across her bathroom mirror. A smashed lipstick lay on the floor, apparently having been used as the stalker's writing tool.

"He was in my bedroom," she said. "While I was in here, he was standing here waiting for me."

He noticed that the hand she had wrapped around her waist was clutching a piece of paper. She saw him looking at it and held it out. The paper shook, and he looked up at her face. She was definitely pale, scared, but she was also trying not to let the fear consume her. He took the paper.

"Jesus," he breathed as he read the words.

To my Lover and Soul Mate,
    After our conversation the other day, I knew I had to see you again.

The way you looked at me, I could see that you ache for me as much as I ache for you when we're apart. I have your photo from the *Entertainment Weekly* interview hanging on the wall near my bed, so you are the first person I see every morning. And at night, I pray to the Lord to bring you to me in dreams, so we can be together even when I'm sleeping.

I wanted to tell you how hurt I was when I saw you kissing Jack Donohue on last week's show. I thought we had talked about how bad that makes me feel. You have enough money now. You can quit that show if they don't listen when you tell them you don't want to be whoring yourself on television for their benefit, that your body is only for me. You must stop it, Sadie. I know you love me. I think you forget sometimes, so I have to keep reminding you. But don't worry, I know you'd die for me if you had to.

I'm going to watch you sleep tonight. By the time you read this, I'll be gone. I just wanted you to know that I've been here, that I will always be here.

Lovesick

"That's actually a more civilized letter." Sadie studied her nails, picking absently at the cuticle around her thumbnail. "I think the message on the mirror is because he heard me talking to you. It upset him. Probably a lot more than my kissing Jack on TV did."

"He's not going to get near you," Patricio said. He knew he could protect her, but he wondered how long she'd let the arrangement go on. Because a guy like this didn't go away—not until he was arrested or killed. And even if he were arrested, that didn't mean he wouldn't come back as soon as the authorities let him go.

"Over your dead body, right, Patricio?" Sadie reached up to pinch the bridge of her nose, as if she had a headache. "That's a scary thought. I don't want anyone getting hurt because of this guy."

"No," Patricio said. "Over his."

I know you'd die for me if you had to.

That statement worried him more than he'd let her know. Lovesick had hit her, he'd broken into her house. This wasn't a delusional admirer who'd go only as far as the law would let him. He wasn't afraid of the law anymore. And he'd obviously go farther than most people expected to possess the object of his affection. It might come to a showdown between Patricio and Lovesick, and Patricio knew he'd kill the man if that's what it took to keep him away.

The question was, would Sadie be able to even look at him afterward?

"I need to work out," she said. "I can't just sit here and think about that letter."

That's when he noticed that she was dressed in a pair of flared black leggings and a purple workout tank, which showcased her cut triceps. She'd slung a towel over one shoulder and wasn't wearing any makeup.

Without cosmetics, Sadie's face didn't have the punch it had on television, but it was striking in a completely different way.

Her mouth was a rosy-pink and her skin had a healthy, fresh-scrubbed glow. And the eyes would always look dramatic, makeup or no, in contrast to her pale complexion and dark hair. In fact, there was a softness to her looks that makeup camouflaged.

Stop staring, you idiot.

She gave him a wan smile and brushed past him, heading for the main stairs. He followed her past countless rooms and down another set of stairs, until they finally reached her workout room. The entire front wall was glass, affording a breathtaking view of the jungle of spiky bromeliads, colorful blooming shrubs, and squat baby palms that surrounded a large, immaculate swimming pool. The back wall was mirrored, and the floor was covered with a short-pile blue carpeting with extra padding underneath. In one corner sat a Universal weight machine and a rack holding several pairs of pink and blue dumbbells in different sizes. Next to the free weights lay a Pilates machine, a large plastic ball, and a couple of yoga mats propped up in the corner. Directly in front of the windows was a state-of-the-art elliptical trainer, a stair machine and a treadmill. Sadie climbed on top of the treadmill, lily-white tennis shoes standing out against its black belt, and started punching buttons on the machine's keypad.

Spotting a folding chair resting against one wall, he picked it up with one hand and carried it to the treadmill. They needed to talk through a few other issues.

Sadie was stretching as he approached, holding one foot against her rear while bracing herself on the machine with her free hand. He dropped the chair and straddled it, resting his hands on the chair back.

"What, you're going to stare at me while I run? What happened to 'pretend I'm not here?'" she asked, her pretty face darkening slightly as she quoted the speech from the night before. "It's kind of hard to do that when I'm worried I'm going to sweat on you."

"Can you talk while you warm up?" he asked, careful to keep his voice polite but distant. "I have some stuff I'd like to— Jeez, Locke!"

She'd pulled the foot she'd been holding up, so it arced over her head, creating a perfect curve opposite that of her spine. Her heel was nearly touching her forehead. "What? Oh, this?" She glanced upward to indicate she knew her extreme flexibility had surprised him. "This is what dance lessons from birth will do to a person. I'm afraid of what my knees and hips are going to look like when I'm old and gray."

Scrubbing a hand across his face— which he had managed to wash at some point during the night—Patricio glanced warily at her leg, then shook his head. Extreme flexibility had its perks, but he didn't think she'd be at all reassured by where his mind had gone for half a second before he'd been able to mentally slap himself into submission. With some effort, he returned to his previous train of thought.

"You told me in my office you were more interested in covert protection."

Sadie dropped her right leg and pulled up the left, first stretching it low to the ground and then pulling it above her head. Before he could stop himself, he started thinking about the ways and places those long legs could wrap themselves around someone else's body. Like his.

Patricio, keep it in check.

"Yes," she replied, oblivious to his runaway libido. "Covert."

Think of the desert. Think of his *abuela* in her floral-print housedresses. Think of anything but Sadie Locke's too-flexible legs.

Her eyes. Look at her eyes. "You understand that without visible protection, your stalker and any other potential attackers are going to think you're vulnerable," he said, mentally congratulating himself on sounding so businesslike. "You lose the deterrent aspect of having a personal security specialist by your side if other people don't know I'm there."

"A 'personal security specialist,'" she said, pitching her voice low to mimic him. "Is that what they're calling bodyguards now?" He just shrugged in response. That's what the Institute where he'd received his training called them, but he didn't care about the title at all.

"I guess with your résumé, you deserve that kind of title, Delta Force." With the touch of a button, the treadmill hummed to life, and Sadie started walking slowly. "And as for losing the deterrent aspect, I understand," she said. "It's just…I refuse to let this guy disrupt my life any more than he has. If I start running around L.A. with some scary-looking man at my side—" She paused. "No offense."

He shrugged again. "None taken." He kind of liked it that she thought he was scary.

"—then rumors are going to fly. My publicist will be fielding tons of phone calls, reporters will be lurking in the bushes outside the studio, accosting everyone they see to figure out what's going on." The treadmill sped up to a fast-walking pace, and she quickened her pace to match. "I don't want to give him that much attention. He's not worth it."

She had a point—one that she shared with many of his previous clients who'd preferred inconspicuous protection. He respected that point of view enough not to push her further.

"Okay." He nodded. "Then I will be your new driver going to and from work or anywhere else in town that you need to go. On set, I'll blend in with the crew. In social situations, I can be a family member, or…"

Untying a purple scarf she'd wrapped around her wrist, she tied it around her head, using it to hold her long bangs out of her eyes. "The press knows I'm an only child with little extended family. You'll have to be a friend, or…" She suddenly became very engrossed in checking the machine for her heart rate reading.

Boyfriend.

"If I'm your date," he said quietly, "it might satisfy the press more. I have a couple of other identities that'll hold water if they fact check."

Looking up at him once more, she nodded slowly. "Yeah, if they're not digging around to find out whether you're my boyfriend or not, they might follow us less when we're out, ask fewer questions." The treadmill sped up again, so she segued into a speed-walking pace, her arms pumping up and down. "Although I have to warn you, the whole media thing around me is never a good time."

"Been there, done that." She looked almost embarrassed by admitting the media attention, and he found himself wanting to reassure her. "This is nothing new for me. I can make them keep their distance from you if you need it, too."

"Thank you." She held up a hand, the other arm still pumping. "I know, I know, it's your job. But thank you all the same."

He nodded and started to stand, intending to let her get on with her workout without him staring her in the face. But she stopped him, calling his name.

"Yeah?" He sat back down again.

"I wanted to know, the security around my house. How did you get through it?"

She wasn't going to like what he had to say, but he knew he should tell her anyway. "I'd recommend a complete overhaul if you want something to keep you safe after our working relationship is over."

That's right, he told himself. It would be over, and soon, if he had his way. He was secretly glad she chose covert protection, though he normally didn't recommend it. Blending in with his surroundings would give him a chance to lull Sadie's stalker into a sense of security. And when the man made his next move, Patricio would be waiting. Lovesick would be dead, Sadie Locke would be safe again, and he could go his merry way and forget he'd ever met her.

"I text messaged Troy this morning," he continued. "He should be faxing you a list of security companies sometime today. If you want to research them yourself, go ahead. Or I can go over them with you."

The treadmill had segued to a higher speed, and Sadie was now running, her footfalls making soft thumping noises against the belt. "What's wrong with what I have?" she asked, only a slight breathlessness to her voice as she ran.

He snorted in response. "What isn't?"

"Okay, so tell me." Thump, thump, thump.

Rising up off the chair, he turned to stare at the pool, its pale blue surface rippling with the morning breeze. "Your front gate is too slow," he told her. "All someone has to do is wait in the bushes until your car comes through and then run inside." He paused. "But I came over the wall."

The steady thumping rhythm of her sneakers faltered for a second. "Are you kidding me?"

He turned and saw she had resumed her former smooth running pace. She glanced at his hands, most likely checking that the skin covering them was whole and not torn up by the glass embedded on top of the wall.

"It's fifteen feet high," she breathed. "With glass." Thump, thump. "And razor wire."

"I came over the wall," he said again.

"Oookay. You came over the wall." She paused, waited for him to go on. When he didn't, she continued. "So then you had to disable the household system. How did you do it?"

"I didn't," he replied. "Lovesick did, and

I followed. He must have watched you enter your security code from the yard, because I first noticed him punching it in. He walked right through the front door. Oh, and your security company didn't wire the patio doors, which is what I discovered when I came in that way, hoping to head him off because I was several seconds behind him. There's a window in the top level of your garage that probably would have yielded the same results. And there are instructions on how to disarm your alarm from the outside on the Internet."

Abruptly Sadie smacked the stop button, and the treadmill slowed to a halt. Her face was pale, and though she tried to hide it, he saw that her hands, which clung to the treadmill armrests, were shaking.

"So what do I do now?" she asked. "It's going to take awhile to get a new system installed."

"Does your house have a panic room?" he asked.

"No," she replied.

"Good." He moved away from the window to stand in front of the treadmill, looking her straight in the eye so she would read the importance of everything he had to say. "You don't need one. The first place women instinctively run to when there's an intruder in the house is the bedroom. We'll have it fitted with a steel door with good locks. And I'm not leaving your side until we catch this guy."

"A panic room." She laughed softly, though there was more fear and bitterness in the sound than humor. "God, who'd have ever thought while I was growing up in Minnesota that I'd live in Beverly Hills one day and be in need of a panic room?"

Before he could answer, the phone rang, its shrill tone making her jump, making him angry that someone had made such a strong woman so fearful in her own home. The look on Sadie's face made him want to wipe the floor with the man who'd put it there. She looked scared out of her mind, like someone who'd been through this scenario too many times before. Probably because she had been.

"He always calls at this time of the morning," she explained, accurately reading the question in his eyes. "He hasn't lately. I just hoped…" She let the sentence trail off. "I'm not answering it. I can't."

Which explained how she'd managed to miss twenty-seven messages left for her last night.

He'd noticed the telephone hanging in the far corner of the workout room when he'd first entered it, so he was able to cross the room quickly and pick it up before the caller hung up.

"Hello, how may I help you?" he answered, affecting a clipped, almost British tone, one a butler or other hired help might use.

A beat passed, then another. "Who's calling, please?" Patricio said, still disguising his voice.

He met Sadie's eyes and he could tell she knew who it was on the other end of the line. Patricio knew, too. He could hear the caller breathing softly, even though the man hadn't said a word or otherwise indicated he was there. Classic stalker behavior.

Patricio wanted to tell the man what he

was going to do to him when he caught him, in gross, exacting detail. But instead, he hung up, keeping up the illusion that the phone had been answered by run-of-the-mill hired help.

Sadie stepped backward off the treadmill and moved to look out the window. "It was him." She seemed almost resigned, as if she somehow deserved to have someone stalking her, threatening her.

"He hung up." Patricio moved to stand beside her, hoping his presence would reassure her somehow.

"He won't talk unless I answer the phone," she said quietly, staring out at the ocean. "That's what he always does."

Patricio didn't say anything, just nodded. She'd told him about the things Lovesick had said to her—the declarations of love, the requests, the threats.

"I always thought I could count on my home being safe, not to mention the studio. It feels so odd to know that neither place is," she continued. She looked as if she wanted to disappear into herself, her tall frame hunched slightly as she rubbed her arms for comfort. Instinctively Patricio wanted to put his arms around her, offer comfort, tell her that everything was going to be all right, tell her he'd keep her safe with everything he had.

Instead he remained still.

Chapter Six

After the fastest shower ever, Patricio came out of Sadie's spare bathroom dressed in a black suit he'd brought with him, a plain black tie hanging over the buttons of his expensive white shirt. His hair was slicked to the side instead of spiked, and his black dress shoes were polished to a high sheen. As he walked toward her, he covered his hair with a chauffeur's cap, and instantly, his entire manner changed. Gone was the tough-guy look of perpetual boredom, gone was the lethal aura that had made her positive he could tear her attackers apart without breaking a sweat. In their place was a polite smile, an easy stance indicating friendliness and approachability. His uniform and manner conveyed pride in a job well done. Somehow, he'd even managed to tamp down the raw, masculine aura of strength-plus-sensuality that usually surrounded him, which was good, because then the women on the set wouldn't be falling over themselves to distract him. By the time he'd reached her, the guy was an unobtrusive chauffeur, through and through.

The only thing that didn't fit with his disguise was the fact that she still felt completely, utterly safe in his presence, diminished though it was.

"Wow," she said, not bothering to disguise the awe in her voice at his transformation. "Are you sure you don't want to be an actor? Because this is impressive."

"No, thank you, Miss Sadie," he said, affecting a faint Irish brogue. "And don't you be tempting me with your Hollywood offers." He doffed his cap, offering her a small bow that would have been perfectly charming if it hadn't been for the amused mockery in his whiskey-brown eyes. "Mike Sweeney of Sweeney and Sons Chauffeur and Limo at your service." He put his cap back on and gestured to the front door. "Now, would herself be wanting a few minutes yet, or shall I go cool down the car for you?"

Okay, he may have been toning down the "do-me-now" vibe he usually gave off, but the Irish accent was kind of hot, fake or no. "I think herself is ready," she said, not without a touch of irony. "And I don't mind if the car isn't perfectly cool." Grabbing her white and black Chanel tote, she moved to open the door, only to have Patricio take it from her. He brushed quickly past her to open the door.

"After you, Miss Sadie." He swept a hand toward her front walk.

She shot him a wary look, half expecting him to morph back into his usual ultraserious alter ego. But he just kept smiling at her in that affable, maddeningly polite manner.

Another Silver Shadow sat in her driveway, identical to the Rolls she'd rode in to his office. Patricio held the back door open for her, and as she got in, whispered in her ear, "Troy made the arrangements yesterday afternoon, after Marilyn hired me. I thought you'd be more comfortable in something you're accustomed to."

She opened her mouth to tell him she'd be more comfortable riding to work on a camel rather than going in that ostentatious car when she met his eyes. He seemed to be laughing at her, and she could've sworn he knew full well that Silver Shadows weren't her style.

"Thanks," was all she said.

As he drove her to Franklin Studios, Patricio told her he'd help her carry her bag inside, and then he'd become one of the crew, melding into the background while she worked. She might not know where he was at all times, he informed her, but he'd be within striking distance at all times, always able to see and hear her.

By the time they reached the gate, Sadie realized she hadn't arranged for ID for Patricio, so she'd have to sign him in as a guest, which was going to look awfully strange, considering he was her chauffeur. Usually her colleagues had their assistants get clearances for their drivers ahead of time, saving them even a moment's inconvenience. But when the security guard approached them, she saw that Patricio already had a security badge in his hand, Mike Sweeney's happy-go-lucky visage grinning in the center of it.

"Top o' the mornin' to ya," he said to the **security guard** as he rolled down the **window. The guard** blinked, muttered a "good morning" back as he looked at the badge, **then** glanced at Sadie. Stepping back, he waved them through.

"Top o' the mornin'?" she laughed. "You sound like the Lucky Charms leprechaun."

"Too much?" he asked in his normal deep voice, glancing at her through the rearview mirror.

"Just a bit." She smiled at him, and though he didn't return it, they rode down to Lot 17 in an easy silence. The whole interaction made her wonder once more why he'd gone to such lengths to set such rigid, impersonal boundaries between them the night before. Because without all that in the way, they would probably have gotten along very well. She genuinely liked Patricio, and it seemed he might just find her easy to be around, too.

Then again, maybe that was just wishful thinking. He was probably the subject of a lot of wishful thoughts with his looks.

She was jolted out of her thoughts as Patricio brought the car to a halt, parking in her usual spot, which she'd described to him a few moments before. She'd been driven to work just a few days before, when her car was in the shop, so it shouldn't seem odd to anyone to see the Silver Shadow again. He got out to open her door.

"Remember, I'm right by your side, even when you can't see me," he whispered as she exited the car, his lips barely moving around his polite expression. "Just say the word, and I'm there."

She could get used to having her own personal security specialist around, especially if that specialist was Patricio. Because she hadn't felt this confident going into work in a long time.

Sadie nodded, barely glancing at him. She started toward the warehouselike building that housed most of the standard

Jungle Raider sets, just as they'd planned this morning. She heard him open the car trunk, take out her oversize Chanel tote as if he were just helping her to her dressing room with her things. And then she heard his footsteps behind her.

Normally she would have walked beside her driver, talking to him as he helped her with her things, but Patricio had told her that the less attention she paid him, the less other people would pay as well. Still, it felt awful divalike to just ignore him like she was.

Keeping to their plan, she walked into the lot building, heading straight for her dressing room, offering good mornings and hellos to cast members and crew as she passed them. And just as he'd said, no one paid any attention to Patricio behind her.

As soon as she pushed through the dressing room with her name on the door, a man dressed identically and with a similar build to Patricio's stepped out of the shadows. His face was more rugged, less handsome than Patricio's, but their height and coloring was similar enough that most people wouldn't notice the difference if they were just glancing at him.

"Top o' the mornin' to ya, Miss Sadie," he said, doffing his cap, making her laugh. "Mike Sweeney of Sweeney and Sons Chauffeur and Limo, at your service."

She turned to Patricio, who had shucked the jacket and tie and was unbuttoning his shirt to reveal a black T-shirt underneath. "Actually this is my cousin, Julio, uh, Sweeney." He winked at her, which surprised her. Patricio obviously was in his element on the job, if he felt comfortable enough to do that.

"I'm a lot better looking than he is," Julio told her. "But no one should be looking at us that closely, especially with this." He pulled his hat down to shade his eyes. "Ms. Locke." Julio nodded goodbye as he walked past her, exiting her dressing room to presumably return to the car. Patricio tucked the clothes he'd removed into her Chanel bag, taking out his beloved combat boots. "I'll be right outside," he said, after hc'd laced them up.

Just as he'd reached the door, someone

knocked on it. Afraid he'd be questioned, Sadie froze, unsure of what she should do. But he nodded at her, silently telling her it was okay to answer it. "Come in," she called out.

Meghan pushed through the door, clutching a pile of letters to her chest just as Patricio became preoccupied with the makeup lamps hanging around her vanity mirror. Meg barely spared him a glance. "Burnt bulb?" she asked, not waiting for an answer before she erupted into her usual torrent of words. She dumped the mail on the vanity, straightening it into a neat pile and not even turning around when Patricio exited the room. "So, okay, here's your mail. I cleared your schedule as much as I could this week like you said, but I thought you still might want to go to the *Overdrive* premiere Friday night—I know how you like Jane Thornton's movies."

Jane Thornton was an up-and-coming director Sadie had had the pleasure of working with on a small independent film that had won the Palme d'Or at Cannes a couple of years back. She never missed one of Jane's premieres—the woman took risks, and as a result, her films were never boring, to say the least. Sadie opened her mouth to thank her assistant, but Meghan just kept right on going.

"Domenico and Stefano—God, I can't believe I'm calling Dolce & Gabbana by their first names—said to tell you they understood about the MTV Awards and asked that you keep the dress for now. They said they designed it with you in mind and hope that you'll wear it to your next important function."

Sadie nodded, figuring it would be a good choice for the Thornton premiere, if she went.

Meghan flipped open her planner, reading from the notes she'd entered. "*Variety* magazine called yesterday. They're doing a 'Women Who Kick Butt' feature, and they're wondering if you would do the cover shoot for it." Sliding her mechanical pencil out of its holder, Meghan tapped one cheek with the eraser end. "Unfortunately Brenda Glaser is the head writer on the piece. I know you hated what she said about you being too over-the-hill to keep playing Jada Winthrop." Meghan snorted. "Over the hill at thirty-four. As if. Sorry again for not keeping that stupid article out of your reading pile."

Sadie smiled at her assistant. "You know you don't have to do that. I became immune to Brenda Glaser's trash-talking a long time ago," she said, though Meghan didn't look any less peeved with Glaser. "Tell them I'll think about it if they give us final copy approval."

Meghan pointed her pencil at Sadie. "Oh, I got you final copy approval already. Not to mention an apology and a giant fruit basket on its way."

Sadie grinned. "Fruit is good." She was about to ask Meghan to tell *Variety* she'd do the shoot when she noticed her assistant seemed to be fidgeting more than usual. Sure, Meghan normally had a lot of energy, but the way she was shifting from foot to foot and flipping the pencil around between her fingers smacked of something wrong.

"Meghan? You okay?" she asked.

Meghan started, blinking once and straightening her posture. "Fine!" She swiped at her face, then fluttered her fingers across her cheek until they were toying with her silver hoop earring. "Everything's fine. Why? Is something wrong with you?" Her jerky delivery was all Sadie needed to know that her hunch had been right.

"Meghaaaan." Sadie shot her a look and waited.

"Ohhhh… Don't do that. You know I hate the Ice-Blue Stare of Death." Meghan shifted her feet and bit her lip, looking decidedly conflicted. "You know, it's really better that I not tell you…."

"I got another letter, didn't I?" For some reason, the thought didn't bother her as much as it usually would have. Maybe because Patricio was presumably just outside her door.

Meghan sighed. "Yes," she said reluctantly. Sliding a thin envelope out of her planner, she made a show of studying the outside of it. "But I really don't think this is something you need to see."

"It's okay," Sadie said. "I took your advice—or Bobby did, actually—and got a security specialist."

Meghan's green eyes widened. "Seriously? Did you convince Patricio Rodriguez?" At Sadie's nod, she put the hand holding the letter over her heart. "Oh, thank God."

That letter really had to be something for Meghan to react as she was. Sadie stood and pinched the envelope between her thumb and forefinger, tugging it gently out of her assistant's grasp. After a brief tug-of-war and with great reluctance, Meghan finally let it go. "I still think I should just give it right to Mr. Rodriguez, boss," she said. "You have to work today."

"It's just reshoots—" she began as she extracted a sheet of paper from the envelope. But what she saw when she opened it made her hand tremble and fear track down her spine like a spider with pointed legs.

He'd pasted a picture of her in the center—or of part of her, anyway. Her head and torso had been sliced out of another photo, and cutouts of miscellaneous arms and legs taken from magazines had been pasted next to the appropriate points at crazy angles. The result was that she looked like a splayed out marionette doing some kind of weird dance. But that wasn't the worst.

He'd taken a pen to her face, blacking out her eyes and her mouth with such angry force, he'd torn holes through the picture. Beneath the whole insane collage, he'd written a question, the same one that had been on her mirror the night before.

Who is he?

"Oh, God," she breathed. She slumped back into her chair, feeling suddenly nauseated. He was angry about hearing Patricio in her house, and now, who knew what he wanted to do to her?

Meghan, who normally never touched her just like everyone else, placed a firm hand on her shoulder. "Sadie, he is not going to get to you." She looked at Sadie in the mirror, using her name for the first time instead of "boss." "Even if he got through your bodyguard, I swear, he'd have to get through me next."

Not knowing what to say to that, Sadie

merely turned around and hugged her assistant, who seemed as surprised by the uncharacteristic show of emotion as she herself was. But you couldn't hear a statement like that without being affected by it somehow. Let the woman sell that to the tabloids—she didn't care.

"Don't you dare put yourself in danger," Sadie said, patting Meghan on the back before letting her go. "I'll be fine. You and Jack told me Patricio Rodriguez is the best there is."

Meghan nodded, though she still looked worried as she glanced at the sheet of paper Sadie had dropped on top of her vanity. "I know, but that letter is just so… awful."

"I know." Oh, how she knew. That was her face he'd mutilated. "I have a bodyguard now. It's going to be okay." As she looked at the collage sitting on the table, she wondered whether it was a promise she could fully believe in.

A few minutes later, Sadie followed Meghan out of her dressing room to head to hair and makeup. Meghan breezed right past the crew member checking outlets in the corridor, but Sadie did no such thing. She slowed as she neared him, the letter from Lovesick folded into a small square in her hand. Her calf brushed his back as she passed, and she dropped the paper, continuing on with barely a glance at him. Patricio caught the paper in one hand before it hit the ground.

She kept walking.

THE MORNING'S reshoots went smoothly, and though most of the time she had no idea where Patricio was, she could feel his eyes on her. It was disconcerting and comforting at the same time, made more so since every once in awhile, she'd catch a glimpse of him in the shadows, checking a boom mike or adjusting a light. To his credit, the other crew members didn't question his presence, even though a lot of them were used to working with the same people, day in and day out. She doubted if anyone even saw him, he was so good at blending into the shadowy corners behind the sets.

After an hour lunch break, Sadie, Jack

and his stunt double Ray Sanders, and Don Cheatham—the actor who was playing the villain for the current season—were to head for a desert area in the Mojave about two hours northwest of Los Angeles. Bobby, the director, had had the crew create an Egyptian pyramid set in the sand, and they needed some sunset on-location shots with a couple hundred extras bundled into Bedouin robes and headdresses.

Back in his Mike Sweeney chauffeur uniform, Patricio drove Meghan and Sadie to the desert set, following the convoy of cast and crew vehicles.

"So, where is this guy?" Meghan asked as they hit the road, glancing around the back interior of the Rolls as if Patricio could pop out of the upholstery. "I haven't seen him all day. I know you said you were getting inconspicuous protection, but is he in the trunk or something?"

With a small smile, Sadie nodded toward Patricio. Meghan squinted at the driver. "Him?"

Patricio met her eyes in the rearview mirror, touching a finger to the brim of his chauffeur cap. Which really should have looked goofy, but somehow, he made it look dashing.

"Shut up!" Meghan exclaimed, bouncing forward in her seat. "You're the bodyguard? And I didn't even notice?"

"Top o' the morning to ya, Miss Meghan," he said in his Mike Sweeney voice. "How is herself doing back there?"

"Herself could use a Diet Coke," Sadie grumbled good-naturedly. Patricio was, after all, not really her chauffeur and therefore, not responsible for stocking the limo's small refrigerator.

"It's top o' the afternoon," Meghan said to Patricio as she sat back. Fishing through her tote bag, she handed Sadie a Diet Coke, then took one out for herself. "The chauffeur is also your bodyguard? That's pretty cool."

"Personal security specialist," Sadie corrected. Patricio went back to driving. Thanking Meghan for the soda, she popped it open and started flipping through the afternoon's script with her free hand. She'd learned her lines ages ago, but it never hurt to reinforce things. Meghan busied herself with her work, and they spent the rest of the drive in silence.

When they arrived, Patricio got out and opened the door for them. Quarter-size replicas of the Giza Pyramids sat in the distance, and much of the low-lying, scrubby vegetation that normally dotted the landscape had been removed. As a result, the sand was a smooth expanse of undulating pale yellow, and with the pyramids in the distance, the smattering of camels sitting on the ground near the lighting crew's equipment, and the two hundred or so extras milling around in their muted robes and headdresses, she felt she'd been transported to Egypt.

As she approached, Bobby ran up to meet her. "Locke! We only have a small window of time where the light'll be just like I need it, so get into makeup, stat. The trailer's over there." He gestured with his gum-chomping chin to a small metal trailer sitting to her right. "As soon as you're done, hustle on over there, by that dune and we'll start with the scene with you, Jack's stunt double, and the camel spiders."

Oh, great. The script hadn't said anything about camel spiders, which she'd heard were the size of dinner plates and liked to run right at you, giant legs flailing. Yuck. Leave it to Bobby to ad lib enormous spiders into an episode that had started with a fairly benign script.

Knowing it'd be futile to argue with him over the spiders—really, she was used to Bobby's creepy crawlies now—Sadie started for the trailers, only to have him bring her up short with a "Locke!" She turned back toward him.

"Tell them to do something with your hair. It's a mess." He ran a hand across his bald head, which was shiny from a light film of sweat. "Someone give me a ball cap," he yelled toward a crowd of crew members. "My head's going to fry out here like an egg!"

After getting her hair and makeup retouched, Sadie left the trailer and headed for the area where the cameras were set up. An extra fell into step beside her, his gray-blue robes swishing around his legs. She looked into his face, only mildly surprised to see Patricio's light eyes peering at her from behind a black desert headdress.

His ease in moving around undetected worried her some. If he could get a costume and blend in with this crowd without an Equity card, the membership card of the working actor's union, could her stalker do the same?

"I know the Franklins," he murmured behind her, apparently reading her thoughts. "They've been making things easier for me than normal. Don't worry." She'd reached the dune where the crew was set up and made a big show of stopping and looking around, so she could continue listening to Patricio. "It's a lot harder for someone off the street to do what I'm doing now," he said.

She nodded, and then he melted into the crowd as Bobby started shouting orders, telling everyone to hurry before "his" light was gone.

She, Ray and Don did the desert scenes four or five times, ending each time with the one where the robed men—minions of Don's villain character—surrounded and separated them, scimitars drawn. Jack's character Tate Ashcroft was supposed to get beat up pretty badly in the scene, which was why Ray was in his place for most of it.

"Ashcroft!" she called to Ray, as scripted, while the Bedouin extras streamed around them, many of them repeating the phrases "walla-walla-walla" or "watermelon-watermelon" to simulate a noisy crowd. "Ash!"

One of the extras came too close, into the wide space around her the actors were supposed to leave for the camera, and he gripped her waist, running one hand up her side before melting back into the crowd.

She swiveled her head in his direction, but she couldn't tell one robed Bedouin from another. "Ash!" she called again, knowing that she was losing focus. The actors closed in around her, the waning sun still seemed too bright, and the crowd seemed to tilt and spin.

Again, someone came into her space. He put his hands on her, his mouth against her ear. "Saaaadiiiee," he hissed. She slapped his hands away, turned around, but once more, he had blended in with the others.

"Ash!" This time, the name was tinged with hysteria, which wasn't how Jada Winthrop was supposed to sound. Somewhere in the back of her mind, she knew she had a line, but she had no idea what it was.

Faces loomed around her, above her. And once more, one of the Bedouins moved against her from behind. "Saaaadiiiieeee," he hissed.

He's here.

She spun around, but the two hundred faces around her were blurring, blending together. They were all hidden by head-dresses in muted colors, all looking at her, all trying to crowd her, to touch her. They were all Lovesick, all intending to do her harm.

Get out of here. You have to get out of here.

Her line. "Ash, hang on! The storm!" she shouted, a cue to the crew to start the wind machines to simulate the dust storm that would provide Jada Winthrop's way out of her latest debacle. On cue, the Bedouins backed off, milling about confusedly while the great fans started to hum.

But before she could break free of the crowd and stop the scene, an unscripted scream erupted from the back.

Sadie spun around at the sound, knowing deep in her bones what was coming, but having no way of stopping it.

Chapter Seven

Seemingly in slow motion, one of the Bedouins ran toward her, having dropped his blunt prop scimitar in favor of a sharp, gleaming knife. The other confused extras parted in front of him like the Red Sea.

Bobby was screaming that he hadn't approved this change in the script.

Out of the corner of her eye, she saw movement, wondered if it was Patricio, wondered if he'd get there in time.

Still the man ran toward her, and no one moved to intercept him.

Sadie bent her knees and crouched low, hoping she could leap out of the way of the knife as soon as the man got close enough. When he was within a couple of feet, she rolled to the left, leading with her shoulder, coming to her feet as soon as she'd tumbled around. Sand rained off her clothes as she stood, turned. A sharp pain sliced along her thigh, and she gasped.

The man was standing right in front of her, a crazed look in his eyes. And the knife was too close. There was no way she could get away in time. He raised his hand, brought the knife down. She held up her hands in a futile effort to stop him.

Suddenly one of the Bedouins burst out of the crowd in a swirl of blue robes, connecting the edge of his curved sword with the back of the man's knife hand. The man shouted in pain, clutching his wrist, but he only had a moment in which to protest. Yanking off his headdress, Patricio swung his blunt prop sword in a sideways arc, hitting the man square in the gut with the flat of the blade. The man doubled over, and Patricio kneed him in the face. As the man stumbled back, his hands moving to hold his nose, Patricio swept a kick at the back of his ankles, causing him to fly backward and hit the sandy ground with a muffled thud. Patricio brought the point of the scimitar to rest in the hollow of the man's throat, the blade no less deadly when used that way, though it was blunt.

"No!" the man shouted. "No, please don't hurt me!" He shrank back into the sand and held his hands with the palms facing upward.

Unable to believe that the man who'd terrorized her for months was this cowardly creature, Sadie moved beside Patricio.

"You're bleeding," he said gruffly, still holding his sword to her attacker's neck.

The pain in her thigh had all but disappeared from the adrenaline high caused by the previous events, but now that it was all over, she could feel it starting to sting again. She looked down to see a shallow but long cut across the side of her leg, bleeding profusely.

"First aid!" Bobby yelled, though his voice sounded far away. "I need first aid over here. Locke! Don't move!"

She stumbled, more from clumsiness than injury, though her leg *hurt*. Patricio caught her around the shoulders with one arm, supporting her until she regained her balance. "I'm sorry," he said, his jaw working angrily. "He should never have gotten that close to you."

When he took his hand away, Sadie noticed he'd left a bloody handprint on her arm. She grabbed his wrist, turning his palm up. He immediately snatched it away, but not before she saw that the man had sliced an ugly gash in Patricio's palm. You'd never know it, though, by the way the guy was ignoring the fact that he was bleeding all over the place. All of his attention was focused on the man lying before them, still cowering beneath his sword.

It must've hurt a lot when Patricio had grabbed her to keep her from falling.

"Hayes, get someone to call the police," Patricio called to the director, and then he looked at Sadie as if daring her to protest. "The time for covert protection is over, Sadie."

She just nodded, knowing there was no way she could avoid the press now, anyway.

With as much feeling as if he were discussing the weather, Patricio turned back to the man. "Now you, my friend, are going to tell us who you are."

Wincing, the man was arching his neck back, trying to keep away from the business end of Patricio's sword. Patricio pulled the sword away and replaced it with his combat boot. Sadie had no doubt Patricio could easily snap the man's neck if he wanted.

"I swear, I've never done anything like this before. He told me to. He told me…"

"Who told you?" Patricio demanded.

"I don't know. He was dressed like all of us. He said he'd give me money." The man put both hands on Patricio's boot and tried to push it off. It didn't budge. "He was supposed to create a diversion so I could get out of here. He was supposed to—"

Patricio applied more pressure, and the man winced. Sadie looked around at the rolling sand hills surrounding the outdoor set. She wasn't sure how the man had planned to get away, seeing as the hills weren't that close. Then again, her dying would have created one heck of a diversion. Sadie shivered, though her brain still wasn't ready to fully process the fact that someone had just tried to kill her.

"Who was supposed to create a diversion?" Patricio demanded.

"I—I don't know," the man said. "He was dressed like all of us. I figured he was another extra. His face was covered, but he had a lot of money on him. He showed me."

Sadie looked around at the sea of half-covered faces surrounding them. There were so many of them here—it could be anyone. If this guy was telling the truth.

Deep in her gut, Sadie knew he was. "This isn't Lovesick," she said quietly to Patricio. "He's shorter, and the eyes are wrong." Patricio scowled at her words.

The man waved both hands at Sadie, as if she could save him from Patricio. "He gave me a prop knife. It wasn't supposed to cut you. It's not my fault. It was supposed to be a prop knife."

Bobby Hayes came over to them, flanked by two burly guys. "Yeah, right, you little twerp. You nearly took her leg off." Which was a gross exaggeration—it really was just a hairline cut. But Bobby's face was flushed, indicating that he was really angry, and she didn't want to get into an argument over the seriousness of her injury with him. For once, he wasn't chowing down on a wad of gum. Sadie wondered if he'd swallowed it during all the chaos.

He eyed her leg, tugging on the brim of the Angels ball cap he'd obviously found to protect his scalp. "Jeez, Locke, get to the first-aid people, would ya?" he said, though his voice had lost some of its usual power. He turned to Patricio. "I called the state police. They're on their way. Bo and Harry here will hold this guy if you don't want to keep stepping on him."

Tossing the sword aside, Patricio reached down and yanked the man up to his feet. He handed the man over to the two security guards, telling them to take him to a nearby trailer, where Patricio would soon join them. Bobby and the guards left, leaving Sadie alone with Patricio—or as alone as she could be with two hundred extras milling about. Fortunately the extras were always instructed to give the main actors a wide berth during shooting, and that seemed to be extending into the aftermath of the attack as well.

She wondered which one of them was Lovesick. And then she shook her head. It didn't matter. She still had little idea what he looked like without a disguise, and Patricio wasn't going to let her look for him anyway—hopefully the police would be able to ferret him out when they arrived.

Sadie tried to look at Patricio's bleeding palm, but he moved it behind him, out of her immediate line of vision.

"You're hurt," she said, remembering full well the deep gash she'd seen there.

"So are you." He gestured toward the cut on her leg, which still stung but had stopped bleeding.

She glanced down at her leg. "It's—"

"—just a scratch," they finished together, then looked up at each other. A corner of Patricio's mouth quirked.

One of the first aid people ran up to

them with a kit in her hands. Patricio took it from her and glared when the woman tried to protest. With a frightened blink, she hurried off, leaving her kit behind.

Sadie snatched it out of his hand. "We need to wrap that up fast," she said, waving the small, metal box at his hand. "You might need stitches."

He smirked at her. "Nah. I've had worse than this."

Walking over to a nearby table, Sadie set the kit down and snapped it open. Extracting a couple of cotton balls and some iodine, she held out her hand. "Let me see," she said to Patricio, who had followed her, as she'd known he would.

To her surprise, he acquiesced, turning his palm upward and holding it out to her. She took it, gently dabbing the cut with iodine-soaked cotton.

"Ouch," she said for him, wincing as she cleaned the cut. He didn't move a muscle.

"It's okay," he murmured. "Just get it over with."

Maybe he was right—the cut had bled a lot, but once it was cleaned off, it looked like perhaps he wouldn't need stitches. Still, it wouldn't hurt to have one of the first-aid people take a look at it, if he didn't scare them off again. She taped the cut closed with the butterfly bandages, then wound some gauze around his hand, which she taped in place.

"The bandages would have been fine," he muttered, poking at the gauze with a look of mild disgust on his face.

"Sure. Let's let some nice sand blow on that and cause an infection," she retorted. "Just don't come running to me when your hand turns gangrenous and falls off."

A corner of his mouth tipped upward in that almost-smile of his. One of these days, she was going to get him to smile at her for real. Maybe even show some teeth.

"Your turn." He took the gauze out of her hands, placing it on the table. She removed her prop gun belt, as he knelt on the ground, his hands touching the outside of her thigh to examine the cut, which was just under the hem of her safari shorts.

Every nerve ending she owned seemed to migrate down to the side of her leg, and it wasn't the cut she felt, but Patricio's gentle touch. He used peroxide on her wound, which didn't hurt at all, then taped it shut with a couple of butterfly bandages. He covered the entire thing with a patch of gauze, which he taped into place, his fingers brushing her bare skin several times.

By the time he was done, Sadie couldn't breathe.

When he was finished, she expected him to rise off the ground right away, but he didn't; instead he stayed where he was as if deep in thought, still on his knees, his hands still on her skin. "I'm sorry, Sadie," he said, his voice so low and soft, she could barely hear him.

"For what?" she murmured.

"I should have seen him coming. This—" he touched the side of her bandage "—shouldn't have happened."

"Patricio." She turned to face him, and he rose to tower over her once more. His face was impassive, but his eyes were so filled with guilt and remorse, she wondered if there was more to his apology than met the eye. "You did see him coming, and you probably saved my life. It's not your fault Bobby made you stand so far from me. I don't think a superhero could have moved faster than you did."

He closed his eyes briefly, the opened them once more. "I'm not a superhero," he said. "I wish I were." And he turned and headed into the trailer where the security guards had taken her attacker, leaving her to follow behind, wondering what that had all been about.

Angrier than he'd been in a long, long time, Patricio grilled Sadie's attacker for what seemed like hours. But either the man was telling the truth, and a mysterious second person had really offered him money to attack the actress, or Lovesick was putting on a really good act. Either way, the guy would be headed for jail as soon as the police arrived.

The only thing he could get out of the guy was the same story—some mysterious man with a covered face had given him a "prop" knife and had asked him to pretend to attack Sadie. He hadn't given a reason—just displayed a lot of money. Obviously the "attack" was meant to scare her.

After their lengthy conversation, Patricio was pretty sure Sadie's attacker had at least a mild mental illness—it was the only thing that explained his ranting, his changeable moods and his motivation for following some mysterious man's vague orders. Patricio did believe that there was a mystery man—Sadie's account of hearing a second person taunting her was no coincidence. Lovesick had been here. Perhaps he was still here, but there was no way Patricio was going to leave Sadie alone for a second to look for him.

Apparently, whoever Lovesick was, the guy was good at picking the weak elements out of a crowd and using them to his advantage. Out of the corner of his eye, Patricio saw Sadie sit down, and when he turned to look at her, he knew that despite her earlier bravado, the man's actions had frightened her to the core.

At that moment, Patricio heard police sirens in the distance, coming closer to the trailer they were in. A few seconds later, there was a knock at the door, and a detective pushed his way inside, holding up his badge. He heard Sadie gasp in surprise when she saw who it was.

"Detective Daniel Rodriguez, LAPD, Homicide Special," he said, and then his eyes met Patricio's. "Yo, Rico."

"There are two of you? Jeez!" the man who'd attacked Sadie said as he looked back and forth between the two brothers.

"Danny Boy," Patricio replied.

His twin walked across the trailer to stand next to him. "You okay?" Daniel asked, undoubtedly because the last time they'd spoken, several armed guards had been dragging Patricio out of the prison.

He nodded, looking away.

Daniel clapped his arm on Patricio's shoulder, leaning in toward him. "If you hadn't said it, I would have," he whispered, communicating in the peculiar verbal shorthand they'd always used, letting Patricio know he was off the hook for his outburst in the prison.

"What are you doing here? Isn't this out of your jurisdiction?" Patricio asked.

"Believe it or not, I was in the area. There's a private forensics lab out here I had processing some evidence for another case. The state police let me tag along when they got the call. Mulvaney has us looking into the break-in at Sadie Locke's house, so I wanted to know if this was related." Captain Aaron Mulvaney was the head of the LAPD's Homicide Special unit, an elite group of detectives to which Daniel belonged. Homicide Special investigated the city's highest-profile cases. And with this second threatening action involving Sadie Locke, they were in prime Homicide Special territory. "Nice outfit, by the way." He indicated Patricio's Bedouin costume.

"Thanks. And yeah, this is related." Patricio motioned for Sadie to come over. "Meet my newest client," he said.

"Sadie Locke," Danny greeted her in his deep baritone. "My wife and sister-in-law never miss your show."

"Thank you," she said politely, shaking his hand. If she'd been surprised earlier by seeing his twin, she hid it well. "Let me know if they ever want to visit the set. I'd be happy to give them a tour."

"Seriously? Thanks. They'd probably explode from joy. Those two are *serious* fans." Daniel took out a pen and a notebook, segueing to business matters. "So, why don't you start from the beginning and tell me what happened?"

Patricio and Sadie gave him a run-down of what had happened, and then Daniel took accounts from everyone in the trailer. After a couple of exhausting hours, where they all felt like they'd answered the same five questions ten different ways each, Daniel and his partner, Detective Lola Ibarra, hustled Sadie's attacker into their unmarked squad car. Then, Danny approached Patricio and Sadie once more.

"None of the extras in Ms. Locke's immediate area saw anything," Danny said to them. "We'll question all of them in the next few days, but I'm not sure it'll yield anything, since their costumes were so similar and the guy's face was hidden."

Sadie just nodded, her arms wrapped around her torso. Patricio wished he'd gotten a good look at the guy, but he hadn't. He'd been moving through the crowd, keeping tabs on the guy who had been getting too close to Sadie, when the man with the knife had attacked. Choosing to deal with the immediate threat, Patricio had lost the man, too.

"He's about five-eleven, maybe 180 pounds, brown eyes. That's all I could see," Patricio told his brother.

Sadie touched his arm. "You saw him?"

Patricio nodded briskly, his mind only filled with his own failure—failure to collar Sadie's stalker when he'd been right next to him, and failure to stop the other man from cutting her. Sure, it had been a scratch, but that had been pure luck. He fell down on the job like that again, she might not survive it.

"That's why you weren't right there when that guy came at me with the knife," Sadie murmured. "No one else even knew something was wrong."

"He's the best there is, Ms. Locke," Danny said agreeably. "There was one time—"

"*Callate, Daniel,*" Patricio muttered. He

really didn't need Danny launching into his greatest hits right now.

Danny laughed. "All right, Rico. I'll let you tell her about your exploits yourself." He turned to Sadie, holding up a plastic bag containing Lovesick's letter. "Patricio gave me this. I'll send it to the lab for fingerprint and DNA analysis. If this guy's been in trouble before, we'll ID him."

She nodded.

"It was great meeting you. I promise, we'll do everything we can to get this guy. In the meantime, you're in good hands." Danny smacked Patricio's shoulder a couple of times, and then his expression turned serious.

"I need to talk to you later," Daniel said.

Patricio looked at him questioningly.

"It's about Sabrina. Joe's got a lead." His brother glanced briefly at Sadie, then back at Patricio. "I know you're tied up here, but call me when you can. Anytime."

And then with a wave, he got into his car and drove off, leaving Patricio wondering whether his brothers really had found their missing sister at last.

Chapter Eight

On the way home, Sadie sat up front with
Patricio, since there was no point in pre-
tending he was just a plain ol' everyday
chauffeur after his Jedi-like display that
afternoon. Meghan said she was catching
a ride with Bobby to talk over increased
security measures for Sadie on set, leaving
Sadie alone with her bodyguard.

As soon as the car was cruising down the
highway, the darkness broken only by the
occasional house or gas station lights, Patricio broke the silence.

"I take it we're on the same page about
the covert protection stopping now?" he
asked.

Leaning back in the plush seat, Sadie
kicked off her sandals. She nodded, but

then realized he might not have seen her in the dimness of the dashboard lights. "Yes. No point in trying to hide anything from the press after today."

"Tell me what you learned."

She turned her head and squinted at his profile. "I don't understand."

"Every time Lovesick approaches you, he reveals something," Patricio said, his voice a low rumble above the car's smooth engine. "Compare this event to what happened in the parking lot. What did you see? What can you tell me about him?"

She thought for a moment. "I think he works at the studio, probably as an extra, although he could be in makeup. Because no tourist would be able to get on set three times, once to get my car keys, once to use them and once to get on the bus with the extras. Not to mention that the makeup job he did to make himself look like an old man was very convincing."

"Good," he affirmed. "If any of those extras have prior stalking records, Danny will find out."

"I'm guessing not," she replied. "The studio runs a background check before it hires an actor for anything."

"Okay, what else?"

She thought for a moment. "He's taller than I am, shorter than you. Maybe about 5'10" or so. He looked like he maybe weighed 180 or so in his old man disguise."

"So we know he's good at disappearing into crowds," Patricio said. "He can sniff out weak elements in a group and manipulate them, as we noted earlier. And he has easy access to the studio and to you. Figure out how he's getting that access, and we'll have him."

Although it wasn't cold out, Sadie still found herself rubbing her bare arms, creeped out by the thought of her stalker having access to her or to anyone near her.

"The letters started six months ago," he continued, "which means somewhere around that time, he was hired by the studio. I can get Danny to narrow down that crowd of extras and the crew using that information, and we might be able to narrow them down even further using the dates of your attacks. We'll get him, Sadie. Every time he comes out of hiding, he makes our job easier."

And he drove her a little more insane. But she didn't say anything like that, because what Patricio had said made sense. She watched the shadowy hills go by, the scrubby tufts of coarse grasses dotting the landscape making them look like they had mange.

The car ate up several miles of highway, during which Sadie's thoughts went over and over Lovesick's letter, the disturbing image of her he'd pasted on it flashing through her memory with stark clarity. She returned to the attack, to the sound of his voice whispering her name in the crowd. And then, when she looked over at Patricio just to remind herself that she wasn't alone in this, something else came back to her.

Sabrina.

Daniel had mentioned someone named Sabrina, telling Patricio they needed to talk to her. Who was Sabrina? And why had Patricio's demeanor become even more withdrawn when her name was mentioned?

Could she be a girlfriend? Sadie didn't know how likely that possibility was, with the hours Patricio kept, but she was surprised to find that she didn't like the idea at all. Which was ridiculous, because she barely knew the man. *And, let us not forget that he doesn't like you.*

The closer the car got to the city, the more she kept torturing herself about this woman. Until finally, she just swiveled in her seat to face him, blurting out, "Who's Sabrina?" before she could even stop herself.

"My sister," he responded.

She couldn't help but feel slightly relieved at the revelation. She waited for him to elaborate, but was met instead with silence.

"I've always wanted a sister. Or a brother, for that matter." She looked out the window, watching the hints of scenery in the darkness go by. "I was an only child. Which was probably a good thing, with my parents."

He remained silent, and Sadie was just about to shut up for good when out of the darkness came, "What about your parents?"

Sadie shook her head. "Oh, they weren't awful. Just overambitious on my behalf, I guess. We lived in a little run-down house in Blooming Prairie, Minnesota. My father was a lumber mill worker, and my mother cleaned houses for a living. At least, she did until she figured that maybe I was her ticket to a better life."

"Stage mom?" Patricio asked.

"Oh, yeah." Sadie was silent for a moment, thinking about all the times she'd just wanted to go out and play with her rapidly decreasing pool of friends in school. But her mother would say no and drag her to one more pageant, one more talent audition, one more lesson. "I was going to auditions or beauty pageants from the time I was 18 months old."

She practically felt him wince in sympathy. "Did you like it?"

"Hated it." She laughed. "Although I have to admit, I was pretty proud of winning the Princess Kay of the Milky Way title at the state fair when I was thirteen."

"Princess Kay of the Milky Way?" There was laughter in his voice. Maybe he needed to be shrouded in darkness to have a normal conversation. Whatever it was that kept him engaged in their conversation, she didn't want it to stop. Not even if she had to keep babbling like a fool.

"The grand prize was a scholarship and your sculpture done in butter."

"In butter?" he echoed, and this time, she could actually hear him laughing. Too bad she couldn't see it very well. Even from the side in that dim light, she could tell Patricio Rodriguez had a killer smile. "Did you freeze it for posterity?"

"No," she said in mock seriousness. "It gets eaten later."

"Nice." And then, just when she thought their conversation was over, he said, "I have two brothers. You met Danny. We have an older brother named Joe."

"Is Sabrina your only sister?" she asked quietly, afraid to speak too loud, afraid of breaking the connection between them.

He nodded, a shadowy movement that she could still see in the dark.

"Is everything okay? You don't have to say anything if it's none of my business.

But if you need to go somewhere, send someone else to be with me…."

"No," he interrupted. "But thanks. I appreciate that." Another silence, and then, "Our parents died when we were young. Sabrina was only a baby. We all were adopted by different families, and only Danny and I stayed together."

"I'm so sorry, Patricio," she said. "Have you found them yet?"

"Joe found us," he replied. "We've been looking for Sabrina for years. Our records were destroyed in a fire, so it hasn't been as easy as it should."

She was almost afraid to ask her next question. "How old were you?"

"Five."

God, she couldn't imagine knowing you had another family out there that you couldn't find, but being old enough to understand that your family had been ripped apart? It was too awful to comprehend. And then he told her about how his parents had been murdered at the order of Amelia Allen, how she might have the key to their finding out where Sabrina was, how she'd refused to tell them when they'd gone to see her in prison.

He told the story with an economy of words, as if he were talking about a film he'd seen or a story he'd read in the paper. She could only imagine what it felt like to go through it.

"I remember when Amelia Allen was arrested. I mean, it was all over the news," she said. "I had no idea that was your family they were talking about."

"You wouldn't," he said, one hand on the steering wheel, the other resting on the ledge between the door and the window. "The news referred to us as the Lopezes, and we wouldn't talk to reporters, so they had to resort to filming the house where we lived as kids most of the time."

She swiveled in her seat, tapping her temple as she tried to remember the news coverage of Amelia's arrest that she'd seen. "No, they caught your brother Joe on Channel 7 a few times." The corners of her mouth quirked upward. "I remember thinking he was kind of cute."

Patricio looked at her sideways, then

turned his attention back to the road. "He's a lot uglier in person," he said.

She snickered. "Oh, really?"

"He has a hunchback you can't see when the cameras are straight on him." He nodded sagely, still looking at the road. "Not to mention that unfortunate skin condition. Scales everywhere."

The last statement made her laugh outright. "Was that a joke?" she asked. "Did Patricio We-are-not-friends Rodriguez just make a joke? Or did I just get teleported to a parallel universe when I wasn't looking? Because that sounded like a joke to me."

"That friends thing," he said, turning his head briefly toward her as the car cruised through the desert. "I acted like an ass, didn't I?"

"Yup," she agreed. "You did."

She heard him sigh. "Sorry."

It made her laugh, though she kept that to herself. So like a guy—no explanations, no excuses, nothing to satisfy her curiosity as to why he'd said what he'd said. Just "sorry."

"It's okay," she responded. And regardless of his motives, it was.

Then, something in their previous conversation came back to her. Before she could stop herself, she found herself asking him, "Were they good to you—your adoptive parents? Did you and your brother have a nice life?" She hoped, she really hoped they had.

There was a moment of silence, and then Patricio reached out and snapped on the radio, putting an abrupt end to their conversation. He turned the steering wheel to take another curve, and the dark, cozy feeling inside the car was gone. Sadie mentally kicked herself for crossing the line, just when Patricio had started opening up. Whether he liked her or not, she had a feeling he didn't talk much about himself. And sometimes a person just needed to.

They came upon a stretch of highway flanked by bright street lamps, illuminating the car in harsh, orange-yellow tones. They were approaching the city.

After a long stretch of silence and road, he finally pulled up in front of her house.

As they entered, Julio, Patricio's employee and cousin who had played her chauffeur earlier that day, pulled up to the gate. Sadie buzzed him in, as she knew Julio was going to take a six-hour shift guarding her door while Patricio slept.

She showed Patricio to the spare bedroom, which had a connecting door with her master suite. And still he didn't say much to her at all as he entered the room and closed the door behind him, effectively shutting her out.

"RICO, oh, God, Rico!"

Patricio ran along the outside of the circle, catching only glimpses of her face as the others closed in around her. He heard the sound of fists brutally smacking on her tender skin, heard her soft "ohhhs" of pain, heard her cry out for him. But still, he couldn't reach her.

His vision blurred, and he fell to the ground, gravel from the warehouse floor digging into his palms and knees. He could still hear her calling him, but he couldn't get to her.

Scrambling up, he tried to shove one of them aside, but the men just solidified into a mass of muscle, keeping him outside. If only he hadn't downed the entire bottle of Stoli in the back of O.T.'s Chevy an hour before. If only he'd known Sonia was going to be here today.

"Sonia!" he shouted.

They were still beating her.

"Stay back, Rico," Johnny Menendez snarled as he shoved Patricio away once more. "You're drunk, man."

Sonia was on the floor now, curled up in a fetal position, her hands protecting her head, her long dark hair falling over her face.

He tried to break in one more time. "Stay the hell back!" Menendez shouted, getting right into his face. Then his fist connected with Patricio's jaw, and Patricio fell to the ground once more.

When consciousness returned, Patricio watched as the circle of men surrounding Sonia spun, around and around, faster and faster, until one by one, the boys shot across the room like pinballs, then disap-

peared. Finally only one remained. In his hand was a broken bottle, glowing green in the dim light inside the warehouse.

"No!" Patricio screamed, but he couldn't move, couldn't think. His head was throbbing, and the alcohol had impaired his balance. He could only watch as the hand holding the broken bottle came down.

And then, that man, too, ricocheted across the room and disappeared. Blood flowed from the wound on Sonia's neck, her skin growing pale and waxy by the second. Her hair turned gray, and her face withered, and the blood pooled on the floor, reaching Patricio, coating his hands, his legs, covering him up to his neck. Still it rose, higher and higher, until Patricio had to swim to stay above the ocean of blood. But something was weighing him down, and he knew it was Sonia, pulling him under.

His last thought was of how desperately he'd wished he could have saved her.

Patricio shot upright, his eyes popping open as he took several deep, gulping breaths, feeling like a drowning man.

As he blinked the sleep out of his eyes,

he saw that his hand was clamped around someone's wrist. Looking up, he met a pair of light blue eyes.

Sadie.

He hadn't intended to sleep that soundly. Sure, Julio was outside, taking over for a few hours so he could get some rest, but Patricio hadn't been able to sleep. He hadn't wanted to sleep, because he'd known what was coming, especially after today.

Another woman. Another failure to protect her. Of course he'd had that damn nightmare, again. And now she was here, next to his bed. Back in that tight gray T-shirt with no bra, the ridiculous drama queen pajama bottoms that hugged her curves in all the right places. She was flushed from sleep, and she looked warm and soft and…

Stop it.

"What?" he asked, his voice sounding a lot colder and more self-assured than he felt. Dammit, he shouldn't have been sleeping.

"You were screaming," she said softly. "I wanted to make sure you were all right."

He let go of her wrist, scrubbed a hand across his face. "Locke, anything that makes me scream is something you want to stay far, far away from." Swinging his legs over the side of the bed, Patricio sat up, fully clothed, except for his boots, which were lined up next to the bedroom door.

Sadie Locke. She surprised him in so many ways. Unlike the spoiled, pampered princess he'd expected her to be, she was warm, kind and even funny at times. And she needed him, trusted only him to protect her, for some reason. So he couldn't walk away, couldn't leave her behind even though he knew he couldn't let her close, either. Because if she ever found out who he was, what he'd been...he didn't want to be there to see the disappointment, the revulsion in her eyes if that happened. And inevitably, everyone close to him found out. *Poor messed up Patricio, what's it going to take to push him over the edge again?*

But the problem was, he'd already started letting her close. He'd told her about Sabrina, told her about his parents without even realizing what he was doing until it was too late.

Might as well have told her you were a worthless gangbanger. That you stole, that you hurt people, that you spent your teen-age years wasted, that you watched your "friends" kill. Get it over with.

But he couldn't say anything, so he just looked up at her, half expecting to already see some sort of disgust on her face. But instead, he only saw concern. And something more.

"What is it? What were you dreaming about?" She sat down on the mattress beside him. For the first time, he noticed she was holding a red ceramic mug in her hands. She held it out to him.

He didn't know how to respond, to the gesture or to her questions, so he just didn't say anything. He took the mug from her and stared at the steaming brown liquid inside.

"Patricio?"

He shook his head, put the mug down

on a stack of magazines on the night-stand. "I don't—"

"Look," she responded, "we're not friends. I get that. I despise you more than the camel spiders Bobby almost made me work with today. Does that help? But I can't sleep, and neither can you, so why don't you drink your tea and talk to me?"

Tea. She'd brought him tea. She wanted him to talk to her about his nightmares, wanted to soothe his fears, stay with him until they left him. He didn't know what to say to that. He'd been a complete jerk to her ninety percent of the time they'd been together, and she'd seen through him every time, through to his vulnerable, scared, selfish core. And she didn't flinch, didn't turn away.

With the exception of his brothers, he'd never felt that kind of acceptance or comfort in someone's presence.

And he'd never felt this kind of heat.

His gaze dropped to her mouth, the full, bow-shaped mouth that had smiled on the covers of countless magazines. He wanted to pull her to him, to cradle the back of her swanlike neck in his hands and run his fingers through her hair, to touch her perfect, ethereal skin. He wanted her, but he didn't dare touch her, afraid that the poison from his past would leak into her present. But, God, he wanted her.

So when she touched him instead, he couldn't pull away.

She reached out, brushing a fingertip along his hairline, pushing his hair off his forehead. He couldn't move, didn't want to. He'd been with his share of women, but it had never felt like this. He'd never allowed it to feel like this, the way one touch of Sadie Locke's hand made him feel.

Her fingertips moved down the side of his face, brushing his temple, across the side of his jaw, until she was cradling his cheek in her palm. With a sharp intake of breath, he bowed his head, closing his eyes and leaning into her touch. Just for a second. Just one more.

"You saved my life today," she said softly. "Thank you."

Slowly, with more regret than he'd ever felt in his life, he closed his hand around her wrist to pull it away. He had to stop this. She deserved more than he'd ever be able to give her.

"Don't you dare," she whispered. And she did take her hand away, though her fingers still trailed along his jaw, the side of his neck. Then, they closed around the material of his shirt. She tugged, pulling him to her, and he couldn't resist her. He moved forward, closer, his eyes focused on that incredible mouth.

Just as his lips were about to meet hers, he pulled his head back. But instead of protesting, she just smiled at him, a warm, wicked, private smile. And he was lost.

"Locke," he groaned, and then he pulled her head down to his.

Burying his hands in her short hair, reveling in the feel of the soft ends at the back of her neck, of her mouth on his, he pulled her to him as he leaned back against the pillows.

She lay beside him at first, then moved to straddle his hips, arching her body into his. Her hands moved into his hair, and she kissed him back with a passion that took his breath away.

He put a hand on her collarbone, gently pushing her back. "Locke, I can't do this," he said, looking her straight in the eye, wondering whether he'd be able to keep pushing her away if she persisted.

Her mouth was swollen from their kiss, and her eyelids were heavy as she looked at him. "You're fired," she murmured.

Moving up to his elbows, he almost smiled at the comment. Almost. He shook his head instead. "It's not like that, Sadie. It's more than professional reasons."

Her face was still, enigmatic, as she moved off him. He'd never been sorrier to see someone move off him in his entire life. And she still had all her clothes on.

"You're a beautiful woman, Sadie," he began.

"Oh, God." She let her hands fall so they smacked her upper thighs and rolled her eyes, obviously believing she knew what was coming.

And I want you. So much.

But he couldn't tell her that.

And neither could he say the words he knew he should—that he wasn't attracted to her, that there were men out there who were better for her than he was, that he thought she was nice, *but*... All the lies he usually told when someone got too close. So, he simply told her the truth, inasmuch as he could.

"You don't want to do this." He swung his legs off the bed and sat up. Resting his elbows on his knees, he looked past her at the wall, concentrated on the uneven pattern of the stucco.

She studied him quietly from her perch at the end of the bed. "Why?" she asked, leaning forward into his line of vision. He saw that her cheeks were still flushed, her short hair mussed. The skin of her neck had an angry red mark on it from where his whiskers had rasped against it. He wanted to do it all again.

"It's better this way. I can protect you, but I can't be anything else for you. I told you that." He studied his hands, knowing that he had to tell her more, that she deserved more. "If you found out who I was, what I've been, we'd end up hating each other."

He expected her to be angry. He thought she'd storm out, or fling back a casual insult at him as she left to let him know she didn't care. He thought he might get stony silence, or one of her too-long stares. He didn't expect her to do what she did.

She pushed off the bed, came to stand in front of him, and waited until, still seated, he looked up at her. Then, she reached out, brushed a lock of hair off his forehead. "It's okay, Patricio," she said. "Whatever you're hiding, you don't have to tell me. But you can." She leaned forward, kissed him softly on the cheek. "Don't be afraid," she whispered, her words an echo of the ones he'd spoken the night he'd started working for her. And then she went back through the connecting door to her room.

He huffed out a breath, a bitter, angry smile crossing his face. Pretty words, but he knew she wouldn't follow through if he did tell her about his past. And if he'd let something happen between them, he would have had no choice but to tell her everything, let her see who he really was, what she'd gotten into.

It was better this way.

For both of them.

Chapter Nine

Although Patricio made it clear to Sadie that he would have been more comfortable with Bobby shutting down *Jungle Raider* production until they caught Lovesick, Bobby Hayes would never have done anything to upset their advertisers. So after only a morning's hiatus from filming after the attack and an abrupt dismissal of all the extras who'd worked on the scene the day before, Sadie and Patricio were back at Franklin Studios.

While Bobby was working with Jack in the part of the lot warehouse reserved for the university library set, Sadie sat in an oversize blue chair in her dressing room, running through her lines. She was dressed in the dust-streaked white T-shirt and khaki cargo shorts she'd wear on camera—she was supposed to look a little rumpled anyway. The chair was big enough for her to rest her feet on the end of the arm, if she leaned back and to the side, and she was doing just that.

She heard the door open and out of the corner of her eye saw Patricio walk inside. He'd gone outside to take a phone call, and she sort of wished he'd just stay out there. It wasn't that things were overly awkward since they'd kissed the night before—they weren't. The two of them were good enough actors that they easily pretended nothing had happened. But when he was easily visible, all she could think about was that kiss, and it was driving her mad. It was all she could do to keep from grabbing the guy and demanding or cajoling or even pleading with him to kiss her again.

But he'd made it plain that there was some reason, something in his past that kept him from getting involved with her. Maybe he was married. Maybe he had a wife in Ecuador or some other exotic location, waiting for him to come home. Maybe he was gay.

Oh, he was *so* not gay.

Without saying anything to her, he sat sprawled in a chair across from hers, his arms resting across the overstuffed arms. And then he waited.

She kept studying her script, but the words began to blur and blend together, as most of her concentration was going toward looking at Patricio without looking like she was looking at Patricio. Finally, unable to see what he was doing and where he was looking, she just gave up and let the book fall into her lap, raising her head.

"Hey," she said. "Everything okay?" He was only a few feet away from her. He was too close. And that way he had of looking at someone like they were the only person in the world…she really had to get over this guy.

"Danny just called me." He drummed his fingers on the chair arm, making a muffled tapping noise. "They got some DNA from the envelope your letter came in."

That surprised her. "They had it tested already?"

"Took it to a private lab in Santa Monica. Danny ran it through CODIS and got a hit." He stopped drumming and waited for her to respond.

She knew from a guest role she'd done on a forensic detective show that the FBI's Combined DNA Index System, or CODIS, was a national database of DNA profiles of anyone who had given the government a sample since 1998. Since it was still fairly new, it was by no means comprehensive, which meant they had to have pretty recent data on the guy.

"Who is he?" she asked.

"David Carpenter," he responded. "Ring a bell?"

David Carpenter. David Carpenter. She leaned her head back, staring at the ceiling. "No. Not at all. I'm usually pretty good with names, but I meet so many people." She sat up straight again. "That doesn't mean we didn't have a chance encounter at some point."

"He also might have just bonded with

you through his television," he pointed out. Then, reaching for a folder at his feet that he must've brought in with him, he opened it and took a sheet of paper off the top of the stack inside. "Picture," he said simply, holding it out to her.

She reached for it, afraid of what she might see. When she held it up in front of her, she was surprised to see that good old David didn't look like a crazy person. He had feathery, sand-colored hair that was seriously thinning on top. His face was a near-perfect smooth oval, no rugged lines or edges to it. He had a slight overbite and a weak-looking lower jaw. His eyes were brown and slightly smallish, tipped downward at the outer corners, and he had a nearly perfect, strong nose.

She shook her head. "I don't recognize him," she murmured.

She never would have pegged him as a stalker, had she seen him on the street. Could this really be her guy? "Why was he in CODIS?" she asked Patricio, still studying the picture. "Prior record?"

"Yes."

The sharp tone of his voice made her look up. Patricio's jaw was tight, as if he were clenching his teeth in anger. "What did he do?" she asked.

He rose, came to stand so close to where she was seated that she had to look up to keep his gaze. To her surprise, he held out his hands, and she gave him hers. He helped her up to standing, but didn't let her go. "I will keep you safe," he said. "Know that."

Something fluttered inside her chest, something cold and fearful. "Patricio, what did he do?"

His expression was intense, his light eyes unreadable. "A woman who hosted a local cable access show in Portland filed a restraining order against him a year ago. Danny's still trying to find out the details, but I think you can guess why."

She nodded.

"He owned a costume and theatrical makeup shop there," he continued.

"Which explains his old man disguise. What happened? How did she get him to stop?"

Patricio paused, his eyes on hers, and she wished to heaven he would tell her already, because it couldn't be any worse than waiting.

She was wrong.

"They found her strangled in her bedroom six months ago," he said carefully.

Oh, God. Six months was when the first letter had arrived.

"She'd been tortured."

Sadie sucked in a breath, gripping Patricio's hands with all her strength, using him as an anchor to keep her here, keep her from running and running and never looking back.

"The district attorney there did everything she could to bury him, but the charges wouldn't stick." His voice sounded so far away, so faint as the white noise building inside her head threatened to drown him out completely. "They didn't get any concrete evidence against him—it was all circumstantial. And he turned out to be related to a state representative with friends in high places. It wasn't too difficult for his uncle to get the case dismissed."

Oh, no.

"Where is he?" She asked the question, even though she already knew the answer.

"He disappeared shortly after the D.A.'s case fell apart," he said. "His family says they haven't seen or heard from him since. No credit card records, but he wouldn't need them. The Carpenters are wealthy people."

All along, she'd convinced herself that Lovesick was just an overzealous fan with no sense of boundaries, someone whose actions might be frightening but who wouldn't seriously harm her. That face, in the picture, it was so normal. It went along with her mental composite of him so well.

But it was all surface. Inside, the man was so confused, so needy and unstable, he'd tortured and strangled a woman in a misguided attempt to possess her. And now he was focused on Sadie.

Without thinking, she reached for Patricio, putting her hands on his strong arms.

"Ah, Sadie," he murmured, and he pulled her to him, holding her close, stroking her hair. "He won't get near you again,

I swear it. He'd have to come through me to get near you."

That's what she was afraid of.

BEFORE HE STARTED shooting Sadie's next scene, Bobby called a dinner break. There'd been such an oppressive feeling in the air between her and Patricio since he'd told her about David Carpenter, she figured they could use a change of scenery. So she'd asked Patricio if he minded going to a hole-in-the-wall diner a couple of miles away from the studio. He'd just given her a look, as if to say it was his job to go where she went.

They were walking to the car—he insisted on taking the Silver Shadow even after his cover was blown, due to the bulletproof windows—in silence when she heard Meghan coming across the parking area.

"Boss! Wait!" Holding on to the hand of a guy who was presumably her boyfriend, Meghan walked quickly toward them. She'd been fluttering around Sadie all morning, her quirky maternal tendencies having gone into overdrive ever since the episode in the desert.

Sadie waited until her assistant skidded to a stop in front of her. "Hey, Patricio." Meghan smiled up at him and then turned back to Sadie. "I wanted you to meet Cary."

Cary gave them a shockingly white smile—the boy had new veneers, apparently—and held out his hand. "Great to finally meet you, Ms. Locke. Meghan says you're a terrific boss."

She shook his hand, told him it was nice to meet him, too. Cary tossed his hair, streaked with meticulously placed California blond highlights, and smiled again, shoving his hands in the pockets of his khaki linen pants. With his Captain America jaw and perfect cheekbones, plus the aqua silk camp shirt that seemed tailor-made to bring out the blue in his eyes, she would have pegged him for an aspiring actor even if Meghan hadn't told her that was the case. She hoped he was a good guy and not one of those self-obsessed, pretty-boy jerks she always seemed to meet on the dating scene.

Sadie introduced Patricio—as her friend, not bodyguard—and then turned to Meghan. "Join us for lunch? We were just heading out to Elba's."

"Oh, Elba's. Love to." Meghan turned to her boyfriend. "Cary?"

"Anything you want, baby." He brushed a quick kiss on her cheek, causing her pale Irish skin to turn bright pink.

Well, anyone who could cause that kind of reaction in Meghan couldn't be all bad.

The four of them got into the Silver Shadow, Cary commenting that he could get used to traveling like that, and headed off.

Elba's was a nondescript, one-story diner on Santa Monica Boulevard a few blocks down from the L.A. Country Club. The squat, pale yellow stucco building with crumbling Spanish roof tiles was nearly hidden by a profusion of thick-leaved tropical plants and bushes that flanked every side of the building. The parking lot was gravel, and the L in the small neon sign over the door had long burnt out. But what it lacked in exterior charm, it made up for with melt-in-your-mouth breakfast food, which it served twenty-four hours a day.

As they entered, a hostess in her fifties greeted them wearing a truly unfortunate-looking uniform—a brown and yellow striped skirt with a ruffle at the bottom paired with a yellow short-sleeve top. The entire ensemble was partially covered by a white apron with ruffles around the bottom and sides. She pushed a pencil into her teased hair as they entered, greeting them with a wide smile.

"Welcome to Elb—Omigod! You're Sadie Locke!" The woman jerked back in surprise, her white orthopedic shoes squeaking on the tiled floor. Patricio moved in beside her, putting himself between Sadie and the hostess before Sadie even realized what he was doing. She touched his elbow. "It's all right," she said when he glanced down at her, so he backed off. Apparently the hostess, whose name tag read Marlene, was new and hadn't yet gotten used to Sadie's frequent visits.

Almost immediately, Marlene brought

herself under control, although her eyes were sparkling with excitement, and she continued to talk a mile a minute. Sadie accepted her stream of compliments as kindly as she could. As always, they were a reminder of how successful the show was, and how lucky she herself was to have such a blessed career. But she always wished people would just treat her like a normal person instead of getting all… sparkly when she was around. If they assumed she was as average as the next person, she'd never disappoint them.

"I just love *Jungle Raider*," Marlene continued as she guided them to their table. "I've seen every episode. You have to tell them to put season seven on DVD already. I'm getting so impatient!" She set down four laminated, single-sheet menus. "Although, dear, you really shouldn't let them do what they did to your hair in 'Eye of Osiris.' I know those pompadour ponytails are in, but I think they just look silly."

Meghan gasped at the woman's forthrightness, but Sadie just laughed. "I totally agree, Marlene. I looked like I was storing food in there." She patted the top of her head to illustrate.

"That short haircut is super cute," Marlene said. "You can keep that one." She winked and touched Sadie's shoulder briefly. "Thanks for letting me blah all over you. I normally leave you actors alone, but my, Sadie Locke." She put a hand on her collarbone and looked up at the ceiling, a contented smile on her face. "You're just my favorite."

"You were great with her," Cary said when Marlene left, his arm resting casually on the back of the booth, fingers trailing on Meghan's shoulder. "Lots of people wouldn't have liked the pompadour comment."

Sadie smiled as she studied her menu. "She was sweet. And the ponytail did look stupid." Raising her eyes, she dropped the menu back on the table. She always ordered the same thing anyway. "Fame is a weird thing. You're in people's homes every week, and they feel like they know you. So they come up to tell you how much your work means to them, or they give you very blunt feedback, or they just approach you to touch you or get your autograph. It can be really disconcerting sometimes, and you can either get mad or you can be Zen about it." Glancing out the window at a car with a bad muffler that had pulled into the parking lot, she laced her fingers together and leaned her chin on them. "I choose to be Zen, unless they cross a line."

Cary leaned back, studied her. "Where's your line?"

She rolled her eyes. "Trying to get a lock of my hair while it's still attached to my head. Groping. Being purposefully insulting. That kind of thing."

He didn't respond. After a couple of seconds of silence, a couple of people approached asking for autographs, which Sadie gave. The waitress came and took their order, and their food arrived in record time.

While they were eating and making pleasant conversation, most of the patrons left them alone, though Sadie could hear some of the customers whispering among themselves and shooting glances at their table. That was something she'd long ago learned to tune out, so she did so.

At one point, she noticed two young men, one dark-haired, one fair, standing on the far side of the restaurant, staring at them.

As she carefully cut a bite-size piece of her lemon-butter crepes, Sadie watched the men through her lashes. Normally she wouldn't have paid any attention, but something about them seemed slightly off. It wasn't the street clothes or the tough-guy poses, either. It was the expressions on their faces. They looked angry.

They moved a couple of steps closer, and the bite of pancake Sadie had just swallowed stuck in her throat.

He's good at finding the weak element in a crowd, manipulating it.

What if Lovesick had sent them? What if they had a message? Or another knife?

Beside her, Patricio's head shot up, as he apparently sensed her tension. "What is it?" he murmured, but she didn't even have to answer. He'd already zeroed in on the men.

They started walking toward their table.

"RODRIGUEZ!"

Seated on the outside of the booth, Patricio didn't even have to lean over to see the man who'd greeted him.

Ah, crap.

A goateed man, who looked only vaguely familiar, flashed the old Latin Cobra sign—two fingers held up like a peace sign, but hooked toward the heart, like cobra fangs. He was dressed normally in jeans and a white T-shirt, though the black and blue jacket was probably his way of wearing his gang's colors. He had two gold hoops in his ears, and about three gold chains around his neck. He flashed the sign again.

Patricio turned away, went back to his pancakes.

"Rico!"

Now Sadie heard the man, and she craned her head around Patricio to see who was calling him. Patricio leaned forward, hoping to block her view with his body, a sick feeling pooling in his gut. Out of the corner of his eye, he saw the man flash the

Cobra sign once more, the gesture tight and angry.

Patricio turned away again, hoping the dude would figure he'd made a mistake and keep walking.

All these years, you never left the city. It had to catch up with you sometime.

But why now? Why in front of her?

The goateed man made the sign one more time, this time throwing it down afterward. Patricio knew the man was trying to insult him and had no idea he couldn't have cared less what happened to the Cobras.

"What is he doing?" Sadie asked him, touching his arm lightly. "Do you know him, Patricio?"

Patricio closed his eyes, wondering how he was going to keep his past from Sadie now, with it staring him right in the face, all decked out in gangster colors.

When he opened them, the man was standing next to their table.

"Rico," he said, disgust making his upper lip curl.

"Look," Patricio said with a calm he

wasn't even close to feeling. "I think you have me mistaken for someone else."

"I don't think so," he said.

Slowly Patricio lifted his knife and fork, cutting himself a piece of pancake. "Walk away, man," he said softly.

"I know you, Rico, you punk," the man said, leaning down, getting into his face. He banged a fist against the tabletop, causing their dishes and silverware to rattle, then reached for Patricio's lapel. "The Almighty Latin Cobra Nation died because of—"

Hooking his elbow around the man's neck, Patricio slammed the man's face into the table. Sadie and Meghan yelped, while Cary scrambled out of the booth and backed away from the fight. The entire room seemed to gasp at once, and Patricio rose with the man, scrambled eggs clinging to his right cheek, in a headlock.

Three younger guys in the back stood up.

"Sadie, Meghan, get out of here, now!" he said. Cary had grabbed Meghan's hand and started tugging her toward the entrance. Sadie, however, was clutching her butter knife looking like a woman ready to throw.

"Sadie, go!" he said. The men were coming closer.

Cary came back for her, and she let herself be led away, still clutching the knife. When Sadie was well out of the gangbangers' reach, he let himself focus on the men coming toward him.

"I'm calling 911!" the manager yelled from the kitchen area.

One of the men let out a loud volley of Spanish curse words, causing several customers to abandon their food and leave, shooting wary looks behind them as they headed for the door.

"I don't know who you are, *vato,* but you mess with Ricky, you mess with all the Spanish Kings." He swung his arms out from his sides, curving his wrists like a rap star. They were all wearing blue, probably the colors of the Almighty Spanish King Nation.

Ricky. Ricardo Ortiz—he'd been a peewee Cobra back before they'd disbanded, about ten years old. So he knew Patricio, and apparently was still carrying a grudge.

"Let him go," the gangbanger said, "and maybe we won't kill you. At least not in the restaurant."

Patricio yawned. "Go ahead."

"Maybe we will."

He had no doubt they would. He'd seen boys like this before. He'd been one.

He just waited.

"Patricio?"

Oh, no. Still holding Ricky immobile, he pivoted his body slightly so he could see Sadie standing behind him, looking, of all things, concerned, and not in the least afraid of the three gangbangers in front of them.

"Come on, Patricio," she said quietly. "I'm not leaving you here."

Swearing quietly in Spanish, Patricio grabbed Ricky by the collar, bringing him up to his face. "If you or any of your friends ever speak to me in public again, I will bury you. You understand?" With that, he delivered a quick chop to the area joining Ricky's shoulder and neck, causing the man to crumple unconscious to the floor. The other three boys were young and stupid, and he dispatched them in short order. Aikido was all about using your opponent's energy against them, and they gave him plenty to work with.

Jeez, they were nothing but boys.

Using his body as a fulcrum, he sent one of them sailing along the aisle between the booths. The next Patricio backhanded in just the right spot on his chin to make him lose consciousness. The third, the oldest of the group, came at him with a gun.

Patricio stepped back, grabbed the man's wrist with lightning reflexes, and twisted until the man's elbow was pointed upward at an unnatural angle. "Leave me alone," he growled, and then with one fast hit using the heel of his hand, he broke the man's arm. He caught the gun before it hit the floor, ejecting the clip and the chambered round, and then tossing the empty gun to the manager.

He'd lost himself again, encased himself in ice. He barely registered the horrified looks of the patrons around him; the groaning man at his feet, holding his arm; the openmouthed stare of the restaurant manager. He didn't want to look at Sadie at all.

Instead Patricio put a protective arm around her shoulders, concentrating on looking out for any friends of the four men he'd just handled as he quickly paid the bill and hustled her out of the restaurant.

Sadie got into the front passenger seat of the Rolls, Cary and Meghan already buckled up in the back. As soon as Sadie had fastened her safety belt, Patricio peeled out of the parking lot, heading back to the studio.

"If you want to stay alive," he said, his hands clenched on the steering wheel, "listen to me when I tell you to leave."

Sadie reached out and pushed a button on the limo's front panel, and a privacy screen rose to block off Meghan and Cary in the back.

"What was that?" she asked.

He kept his eyes on the road, feeling the cold inside him starting to slip at the sound of her voice. "A dangerous situation you should have avoided."

"Did they…know you somehow?"

He remained silent. *Don't make me tell you.*

"Patricio, talk to me. Whatever it is, I don't care."

"Trust me, you don't want to know," he said, his voice harsher than he'd intended. It was enough to make her drop the subject. But he knew it was just a matter of time before she figured him out, found out about his past.

There was nothing he could do about that. He was who he was, for better or worse.

But he'd think about her for the rest of his life, long after she'd forgotten him.

It was better that way.

They rode the rest of the way in silence. As they passed through the Franklin Studios gate, the ironwork "FS" logo above their heads, Sadie turned to him once more. "When you told that guy to go ahead and kill you, were you just baiting him," she asked, "or were you serious?"

At the moment, he didn't have an answer for her.

Chapter Ten

She'd pushed him too far.

After Sadie had finished the day's shoot-ing, Patricio had driven her home, refusing to speak to her in anything other than monosyllables. When they'd gotten there, Julio was waiting for her, along with an-other Rodriguez and Associates "associate" named Ren, who'd told her he was half-Japanese, half-Cuban, and former Secret Service.

As Patricio left her in the care of two bodyguards, apparently not trusting just one, he explained he'd be with his broth-ers, finding out what they knew about Sa-brina's whereabouts.

Even though he and Danny had been playing phone tag since that day in the desert, when Danny had mentioned they had a lead on their sister, she knew it was just an excuse. He just wanted to get away from her.

Sadie walked into her bedroom and shut the door, knowing Julio and Ren wouldn't follow her in there. She sat in an over-stuffed chintz chair that matched the one she'd set outside for Patricio. That night seemed like it had been ages ago.

She stared blindly out the window at the front yard. She kept catching glimpses of his past—the murder of his parents, the adoption, his formidable résumé. Those pieces he hadn't been afraid of her scrutinizing. But somewhere in between there was a black hole that he kept trying to hide.

What is it, Patricio? What are you so afraid I'll see?

Those men in the restaurant had called him Rico, just like his brother Daniel. Therefore, they really had recognized him, even though he'd told them they were mistaken. And she knew a gang sign when she saw one. She hadn't heard of the Cobras, but maybe that's because she'd been lucky enough to avoid most of the areas of Los Angeles where gang activity was prevalent.

It usually wasn't prevalent at Elba's. At least, not to her knowledge. But there had been gangbangers there yesterday. And she hadn't been able to stop thinking about Patricio's reaction to them ever since. *Go ahead.* She'd seen the look in Patricio's eyes when one of those men had threatened to kill him, when he'd dared the man to do it. And it had frightened her to her core, more than Lovesick ever could.

It made sense, in a way. The extreme sports, the daredevil résumé, the way he pushed everyone away almost immediately upon meeting them. Patricio Rodriguez didn't care whether he lived or died. And something in his past was the key to knowing why.

Without stopping to think about what she was doing or why, she made a phone call to her alma mater, St. Xavier University. Then, she waited in her room until it had been dark for several hours before heading out to St. X. Julio and Ren didn't seem to mind heading out at that hour, though she guessed they wouldn't tell her if they did. Well, it was an emergency, so either way, they'd just have to deal.

St. Xavier had been a great experience for her—she often credited the professors in the theater department for her successful transition from child actress to adult A-lister. And she'd made several hefty donations each year since her graduation to show her gratitude. She never liked to call in favors in return for gifts, but it was worth making an exception, just this once.

When they reached St. X, she parked the Civic as close to the Thomas More Library as possible. Julio and Ren followed her silently down one of the sidewalks crisscrossing the green space in the center of campus known as the Quad. The library was a modern building, constructed of a warm, yellow stone with large towering windows and glass front doors that allowed you to see the activity near the front desk. When she pushed on those doors, she found that, as promised, they were unlocked, even though it was just after closing time. She went in, Ren coming with her and Julio staying outside.

A woman who was most likely the head librarian she'd talked to on the phone sat at the front desk, tapping on a computer keyboard with the eraser side of a pencil. She wore a red satin button-down shirt paired with a forties-style tweed fishtail skirt. Her glossy black hair was pulled back in a ponytail, so her curls fountained over the top of her head. Standing behind her looking over her shoulder was one of those woman who made elegance look easy, her caramel-brown hair cascading over her shoulders in that carefree, shampoo-and-go way that would have taken a team of stylists hours to mimic on Sadie's hair.

The two women looked up as Sadie stepped into the main lobby, Ren just behind her. The brunette pulled off a pair of tortoiseshell reading glasses she'd been wearing and hooked them into the neckline of her beige wide-weave summer sweater, a welcoming smile on her face.

"Well, hello, Ms. Locke." The curly-haired woman who'd been typing stood and identified herself as Celia and confirmed that she was, indeed, the head librarian. "How can I help you?"

"It's Sadie. I just wanted to look through your *L.A. Times* archives for a few minutes." She glanced at the round black-and-white clock that hung over the library's central staircase to the second floor. "I won't keep you too long, I promise."

Celia waved a hand at her with a *pffft*. "It's no trouble. I'd rather stay a little later for you than have a mob scene in here with your fans on campus." She tilted her head back, indicating the woman behind her. "Oh, and this is my sister-in-law, Dr. Emma Reese Lopez from our literature department, in case you're searching for any obscure eighteenth century poets."

Emma stepped forward to shake her hand, her silk pants flowing as she moved. "Actually I'm a huge fan, and the two of us were shrieking like idiots when we heard you were coming," she said.

Celia shot her sister-in-law a wide, conspiratorial grin. "Yeah, we never miss *Jungle Raider,* and it's pretty much all we can do to keep it together and not fall all over ourselves right now. I'm sure you get enough of that."

Sadie laughed, immediately feeling at ease with the two women. She was glad she'd made that phone call after all.

Back to business, Celia waved a hand toward the back of the library. "The microfilm machines are right where they were when you were a student here. I'll walk you back there. Can I get your, uh, friend anything?" She glanced at where Ren was standing next to the door, looking about as inconspicuous as the president's security detail, standing at parade rest near the library's double doors. At least he wasn't wearing sunglasses at ten-thirty at night.

"Ren, do you need anything?" Sadie called to him.

"No, ma'am," he responded. They were really going to have to work on that "ma'am" thing. Why couldn't people just call her Sadie?

She turned toward the microfilm projectors, Celia and Emma falling in companionably at her side. "May I ask what you're researching?" Celia asked as they made their way through the stacks. "I might be able to help." She held her hands out in front of her, palms out. "Just tell me if you'd rather I took a flying leap off your universe instead."

Sadie laughed again. "This is going to sound weird, but I wanted to check the *Times* for articles on what happened to this street gang called Latin Cobras. They're—"

"Oh!" Celia stopped in her tracks, causing Emma, who had fallen slightly behind as she skimmed the bookshelves, to nearly bump into her. "Sorry, you just surprised me," Celia said. "Yeah, I know the Cobras. I can definitely help you with that."

"She probably doesn't need to check the indices, either," Emma murmured, pulling a copy of *Northanger Abbey* off a shelf just above her.

Before Sadie could question their statements, Julio appeared in the stacks behind them, apparently having checked out the outside of the building already. Celia blinked in surprise when she saw who he was. "Julio?"

"Hey, Cel, Emma," he said, nodding at them in greeting.

"What are you—?" Emma started to ask, but then she made the obvious logic leap. "Oh, bodyguards." She turned back to Sadie. "You went to Rodriguez and Associates."

"Get out!" Celia also spun to face Sadie, waiting for confirmation.

Sadie nodded. "Long, stupid story, but yes, I did. It's just temporary." She hoped. They'd reached the machines, which sat in a row behind a large research table. "You know of them?"

After circumventing the table, Celia reached out and hit the on switch of the nearest one, causing the fan inside to hum as the light came on behind the small screen. "Believe it or not, we're married to the owner's brothers." She picked up a dictionary someone had left near the machines and tucked it under her arm.

"Joe and Daniel?" Sadie asked before she could stop herself.

A small smile played at the corners of Emma's mouth as she leaned back and sat on top of the research table. "She's met Patricio."

"And she knows about his brothers, which means he actually had a normal conversation with her instead of pulling that silent, deep-and-misunderstood thing of his." A wide, slow grin spread across Celia's face as she waited for Sadie to respond.

"Patricio was working for me, but he had to go out of town," she said, wondering why they were looking at her in that knowing way, in between shooting amused glances at each other. "And I met Daniel yesterday. He's very nice."

"He didn't tell me," Celia said, "for which I may have to smack him."

With a laugh, Sadie turned to the cabinets lined up just past the microfilm projectors, each labeled with their contents. In between the machines and the cabinets was a small bookshelf containing large, heavy-looking books bound with nearly identical red covers embossed in gold. "The *L.A.*

Times indices are still here, right?" she said.

Celia slipped past her and pulled the index for 1991 off the shelf, hefting it onto the table with an "oof." "So…" she said.

"What do you think of him?" Emma finished.

Okay, those two were definitely getting weird. "He's—" She stopped, having no idea how to finish that sentence. *Amazing. He's scary as all get out. He has more of a conscience and a sense of right and wrong than anyone I've ever met. His eyes are gorgeous, and they make my knees weak, and I can't remember the last time I've felt like that when I've kissed a man. He makes me feel safer than I've ever felt in my life. And I'd give anything to heal whatever it is he's carrying around inside him, if only he'd just talk to me.* "—great," she finished lamely.

Celia and Emma just looked at each other again. Then, Celia reached out and cracked open the heavy red book on the table, flipping through the pages and running her finger across the entries until she found the one she wanted. "Latin Cobras. Here you go." She shoved the book in Sadie's direction, her expression serious now.

Sadie glanced at the page. Sure enough, there were several listings for the street gang.

"Just yell if you need anything," Emma said, and the two women turned away to leave.

They'd just reached the end of the table when Sadie stuck her hand under the front cover of the index and thunked it closed. "Wait," she said. "Please."

Emma and Celia returned, ending up on either side of her. Celia sat down next to Sadie, while Emma simply leaned against the edge of the table, arms folded. Both wore nearly identical expressions of curiosity and concern. Julio still stood near the stacks, close enough to get to Sadie if he needed to but far enough away that she could pretend he couldn't hear her speaking.

God, she couldn't do this. She had no idea what to say, except to apologize for making Celia stay late on a weeknight for nothing. She reached up and tangled her hands in her short hair, resting her elbows on the tabletop. "I don't know what I'm doing here," she muttered.

Biting her lip, Celia put a comforting hand on Sadie's shoulder. "I know this is none of my business, but are you and Patricio...involved somehow? He just doesn't talk about his family to anyone, generally. And with you looking up the Cobras..." She let the question trail off.

Sadie considered the question for a moment. Her instinct told her she could trust Celia and Emma, but years of getting burned at least half of the time when she confided in someone made her keep quiet.

Something in her expression must've betrayed her thoughts, however, because Emma sank down in a chair beside her. "We're really not trying to pry, but you can trust us. We've been where you are right now."

Celia snorted. "Oh, *yeah* we have." She clasped her hands on the table and looked earnestly at Sadie. "The Rodriguez-Lopez men are like their own force of nature. Normal laws of the universe don't apply."

Sadie pressed the heels of her hands against her eyes, wishing she could just snap her fingers and make the whole mess go away. She was starting to feel embarrassed by her reasons for being here. "We're not involved," she said. "Not really."

Emma and Celia got so quiet, she took her hands away and peered at them. They were a study in feminine sympathy, both looking at her like she was a time bomb about to explode.

Emma leaned one elbow on the table, tilting her head toward it so she could reach her hair to toy with it. "Do you want to talk?"

"We promise not to say anything," Celia interjected. "I mean, you could end up marrying Patricio and then spilling every ugly family secret about us on the *Tonight Show* or something."

"Well…" It was so tempting, to just have a girlfriend moment and get it all out. And then, Sadie just decided heck with it. At worst, they could tell the tabloids she was falling for her bodyguard, which was hardly earth-shattering news. Or, they could tell Patricio himself. And after that kiss they'd shared the other day, he could hardly be shocked. "I just…I wish he'd just talk to me."

Emma nodded sagely as she twirled her hair. "We know."

"I mean," Sadie continued, "Patricio wouldn't be Patricio if he sat down and emoted on a regular basis, but throw me a bone, you know?"

Celia snickered. "Oh, we know."

"One minute, he's looking at me like I'm the center of his universe." Sadie leaned back in her chair, crossing her arms and stretching her legs out under the table. "And the next, he's pushing me away with everything he has."

"We know!" Celia and Emma said in unison. "Jeez, I could write a book on that," Celia added.

"But when he kissed me, it was…" Sadie paused, trying to think of the best word to complete that sentence. "Right," she said. "Perfect. Amazing."

Both women sighed. "Oh, yeah, we know that, too," Emma said.

"But once, we were driving back from a shoot, and he actually opened up," Sadie said. "That's when I found out he had brothers. He told me about Sabrina—"

Emma lightly smacked the table with both hands in surprise. "He told you about Sabrina?" she asked.

Sadie nodded. "Yeah."

"Weeeeell," Celia flashed that amazing grin of hers again. "Methinks our Patricio has finally met his match." When Sadie shot her a puzzled look, she just twirled her hand at the wrist. "Continue, please."

Realizing Celia wasn't going to clarify that statement, Sadie obliged. "But there's something in his past that's causing him to push me away, I know it."

Emma cleared her throat abruptly.

With a glance at her, Sadie reached out and pushed the index farther away from her with both hands. "Something happened that made me think the Latin Cobras might have something to do with it. But—" She shoved a hand through her hair and sighed.

"I'm prying. Because he won't open up to me, I'm digging into something that is none of my business, and I'm not even giving him the choice about it."

"Believe me," Emma said, "we understand. And I think I got the brother who's most forthright about his emotions."

"But you're right," Celia said. "It's Patricio's place to tell you." She tapped the book with two fingers. "You shouldn't find out like this. Although I can tell you you're on the right track."

"Just remember, when you do find out, what happened in Patricio's past is past," Emma said. "He's so much more today. He's a good man."

"Yes, he is," Sadie responded. Then, placing her hands flat on the table, she pushed herself up to standing. "I'd better get out of here before I cave to temptation and start tearing through your microfilm cabinets. Thanks so much for opening your library to me. I appreciate it. And thanks for the talk."

Emma laughed as she and Celia rose as well. "Our pleasure," she said.

Instead of moving around the table, Celia turned to face her, her expression serious. "Being married to the person closest in the world to Patricio, I have one piece of advice for you," she said. "If you really care about him, if you really think this could be something between you two, make him tell you about his past. Push him to the wall. Never let him forget what he is to you, and make him realize how important you are to him. Because even from the little you've told us, I think you are. He never talks about Sabrina to anyone but his brothers."

Emma nodded in agreement. "All I can get him to talk about are extreme sports and basketball."

Celia's forehead furrowed. "No, there was that one time when he talked to us about how ugly he thought Joe's dog was."

"That's how we know he loves us," Emma said. "He confides in us about the important things."

The three of them finally moved around the table and into the stacks, Julio following behind at a discreet distance looking like he hadn't heard a thing, God love him.

"You do care about him, don't you?" Celia asked. "I mean, you seem to, but he's family. We have to ask."

Now, how did she answer that? Sadie took a deep breath as she studied the ceiling. "Anyone who reads *People* magazine probably knows my dating history better than I do," she said carefully, "but for the first time in my life, I think I'm—" *Oh, God.* "—falling in love."

She felt Emma and Celia put their arms around her shoulders. "Cool," Celia said with a smile.

IT WAS JUST AFTER midnight when Sadie finally walked into her home, Julio and Ren close behind. They told her they'd take turns catching some sleep, so, after making sure they were both as comfortable as possible, she escaped into her bedroom for some much-needed rest.

But as soon as her head hit the pillow, she couldn't sleep. Again and again, her thoughts turned to Patricio, and to the conversation she'd had about him with Celia and Emma.

You're on the right track.

So he had been involved with the Cobras somehow. But what had happened, what was so awful that it caused him to push everyone away years later? She was mostly ignorant about what went on in city gangs, but she knew the basics—fighting, drugs, drinking, sex.

Murder.

No, Patricio hadn't killed anyone. That much she knew. As for the rest of it, she wouldn't think about the particulars until she heard from Patricio himself.

The phone rang, startling her. She shot up into a sitting position on her bed, grabbed the phone on her nightstand.

"Patricio?" she said, hoping to heaven it was him.

"Yeah," he whispered. She could barely hear him, there was so much static on the line. "Sadie, I'm in trouble."

Her heart lurched into triple time. "Patricio, where are you?"

"Open the gate, Sadie. Please."

Kicking the covers off her legs, she scooted off the bed, headed for the door. "I'll be right there."

She burst through her bedroom door, startling Ren, who'd taken his place in the chintz chair still sitting outside her door. He'd barely gotten to his feet when she was running down the stairs, her bare feet smacking against the wood. By the time Ren made it to her side, she'd smacked the button to release the gate, had unlocked the front door. She threw it open.

"Sadie," Ren said, a question in his voice.

Patricio stood in silhouette in the middle of her yard, no car in sight. She could see he had on jeans and a dark-colored collared shirt, untucked. She could see his tousled hair, his usual easy stance, shoulders thrown back, feet apart. But because of where he stood, the moon and streetlights behind him, she couldn't see his face, and that one detail caused the hair on her neck to prickle.

She was being so stupid. It was Patricio.

She stopped on the edge of the landing, Ren close behind her. "Patricio? Why don't you come inside?" she called.

"Come here," he said.

"Rico?" Ren said. "What's going on?"

Patricio looked over his shoulder, and his profile…

"I think there's someone in the house."

You can't protect yourself against an enemy you can't see.

"Ren," he continued. "Go inside and get Julio. I'll take care of Sadie," Patricio said.

"You're scaring me," Sadie said. Ren paused, staying by her side. There was just something…

"Sadie, get over here!" he said sharply, and his low voice pitched upward, just for a second, just long enough for her to be sure.

It wasn't Patricio.

Chapter Eleven

Sadie gripped Ren's arm. "That's not him. That's not Patricio. He's a mimic." She'd barely gotten the words out when Ren's arm shot out and he swept her behind him, propelling her through the doorway with his body between her and the man who had to be Lovesick.

"Julio!" he called, following her inside. She heard noise coming from upstairs as Ren whipped out a cell phone and started dialing. He handed her the phone. "Tell the police there's an armed intruder outside," he said.

Armed?

Within seconds, Julio was downstairs, shirtless, but gun in hand. "Take her into the back of the house. Don't go near the windows," Ren told him.

Bang!

A sound like a body slamming against the door made her jump. Julio put himself between her and the door, guiding her toward the back of the house, as Ren had instructed. They ended up in the downstairs bathroom, which had no windows except for a skylight above but was more than spacious enough for the two of them.

Still clutching Ren's cell phone, she dialed Patricio's number. He answered on the first ring.

"Rodriguez."

"Patricio, oh, thank God. Where are you?" She was so relieved to hear his voice, she didn't even try to disguise it.

"LAX. What's wrong?"

Sadie had known she'd been right about the guy outside not being Patricio, but to hear him confirm it frightened her even more. The disguise had been so convincing, down to his posture, and the voice… "There's someone… Oh, God,

Patricio, he's outside. He looked and sounded just like you."

She heard him swear under his breath. "I'll be right there."

THE MAN had disappeared in the time it had taken Ren to call Julio down from the spare bedroom. When Patricio arrived, he didn't say a word to her at first. He gave Julio and Ren instructions on how to thoroughly search her property and, once they had gone outside, he went through the house. One of his preferred companies had come through and installed a new security system around the house—there was nothing to be done about the gate, but apparently he wasn't going to rest until he'd checked every possible entry point himself. He kept her with him the entire time, even after the police arrived.

It took awhile for them all to give the two detectives who arrived—not Danny and Lola but Homicide Special nonetheless—their statements, and then, finally, the police left.

Sadie should have been exhausted, but

she wasn't. Ren went into the spare bedroom upstairs, and Julio took his turn in the chintz chair.

And Patricio was right by her side, where he stayed, even when she'd walked into her bedroom. He stood in the middle of the room, his jaw working furiously. She didn't know if he wanted to yell at her or punch something, but she fully expected whatever his next act was to be violent. She closed the door, her hands still holding onto the knob behind her.

Eyes smoldering, he crossed the room in two strides, until he was standing right before her. "Sadie," he said, taking her shoulders in his strong hands. "God."

And then he kissed her.

The sheer emotion behind that kiss literally made her knees weak, but he caught her when she faltered, his arms around her, supporting her weight, and his hands...oh, his hands.

They were in her hair, on her face, tracing her spine, and his mouth was raining kisses on her jawline, her cheeks, capturing her mouth again, teasing her with his tongue. His body pinned hers to the door, and she was making sounds that she knew Julio could probably hear, but she didn't care.

And then he pulled away.

"Sadie," he murmured, his full mouth already swollen from kissing her, his eyelids heavy.

She grabbed the lapels of his black button-down shirt in one hand, pulling him back to her. "Don't you dare," she whispered, and then his mouth was on hers once more. Her hands started working on his buttons.

"Are you sure?" he murmured into her mouth, and she kissed him again.

"Oh, yes," she said.

In one economical movement, he shucked his shirt, and she ran her hands up his flat stomach, his incredible pecs and broad shoulders. She couldn't touch him enough, couldn't get close enough. Catching the hem of her T-shirt, she pulled it up over her head revealing the shell-pink La Perla bra underneath.

He inhaled sharply. "You're beautiful."

He reached out and lightly traced her collarbone with the back of his fingers, his eyes skimming down her body. Then his mouth followed his hand. "You're so beautiful." He kissed her neck, then made his way down her body, between her breasts, down her stomach, until he was on his knees before her. She braced her hands on his shoulders to keep herself standing.

He hooked his hands into the waistband of her cotton skirt, tugging it gently over her hips, down her legs until it pooled at her ankles. And then his hands were on her, skimming the back of her legs, the inside of her thighs, going places that made her moan and dig her nails into his shoulders to keep from falling.

"Patricio," she gasped. "Come here. Please come here."

He rose to tower over her once more, a wicked smile on his face. "What do you want, Sadie?" His bare arms wrapped around her waist and he pulled her to him, making her gasp again at the delicious sensation of his skin on hers, her body against that incredible chest. He leaned over, taking her earlobe in his teeth. "Tell me what you want," he murmured.

"You." She plunged a hand into his soft hair, the other clinging desperately to his arm. "I want you. Right now."

He laughed softly. "You're the boss," he said. And then he scooped her effortlessly up into his arms and carried her to the bed.

She lay back against the pillows, and then his body was on top of hers, and he was kissing her again, taking her breath away.

It was all she could do to pull away. As soon as he felt her resistance, he stopped, rising above her on his arms, a question in his eyes.

"What do you want, Patricio?" she asked.

The look he gave her was heartbreakingly sweet, an expression she'd never before seen on his normally hard face. She reached out, cupped his cheek. "You, Sadie Locke," he said. Then he leaned into her touch, closing his eyes. "I don't think I've ever wanted anything more in my life."

Reaching up to cover her hand with his, he leaned down and kissed her softly, with a gentleness that nearly undid her. And then he made love to her with a passion that took her breath away.

SADIE LAY *crumpled in the middle of the floor, her short hair swirling in her eyes as blood pooled underneath her head. One arm was stretched toward him, palm turned upward, fingers curling in.*

"Sadie!" he screamed, but she didn't move, didn't even breathe. Latin Cobras circled around him, blocking his path, solidifying into a wall of bodies that wouldn't let him through.

"Sadie!" He pushed against them, looking for a weak point. Someone turned the lights on inside the warehouse, and the brilliance dazzled him for a moment, making him close his eyes. When he opened them again, he saw a ray of light coming through the circle where two people had left him an opening. He lunged for it, diving through.

He ended up on his hands and knees, blood pooling around him. Reaching for

Sadie, his hands closed around a thin, bony wrist. When he looked down, he saw that he was holding a skeletal hand. When he looked up, he saw a skull grinning back at him, the skeleton it was attached to sitting up, wearing Sadie's clothes.

He scrambled to his feet, backing away. His body smacked into another, and when he turned around, he saw that the circle of Latin Cobras was still there, leering at him, taunting him, though he couldn't hear what they were saying.

Every single one looked just like him.

HE HEARD someone calling his name, felt a pair of hands on him.

"Get away," he rasped, half awake, half dreaming. He pushed the hands away.

"Patricio, I'm here. It's all right. Wake up."

This time, when he felt her touch him again, he clung to her. "Sadie?" He opened his eyes.

He was standing in the middle of the room, and she was right there, wrapped in a sheet, rubbing his arm.

He scrubbed a hand across his face, wiping the sleep out of his eyes. "Sorry," he said, moving to sit on the edge of the bed.

Sadie sat down beside him. "Do you ever sleep through the night?" she asked.

He gave a short, bitter laugh. "No."

She put a hand on his arm again, her expression pure concern. "Patricio, what is this?"

He could have played dumb, could have pretended not to know what she was talking about, but he couldn't do that to her. Not now.

Reaching out for him, she put her hands on his face, turning it toward her. "I'm falling in love with you."

Whoa. He'd expected her to say a lot of things, but that wasn't one of them. But almost immediately, he knew, with a clarity and a certainty he'd rarely felt in his life, that he was falling for her, too. And he wished to God that he could tell her that.

"I know I'm practically begging for you to rip my heart out by saying that, but I don't think you will," she continued, still touching him. "I wanted you to know how much I love and admire and respect who you are, right now, this minute. Whatever it is in your past that you're trying to hide, it isn't who you are now. And there's nothing you could say to me that would change the way I feel about you."

He put his hands on her wrists, pulled them away from his face and just held them, staring at their entwined fingers. "You know those gangbangers we saw at the restaurant?"

She nodded silently.

"One of them was in the Latin Cobras, a street gang that used to hang out in East L.A., not far from where my second family lived." He took a deep, shuddering breath as words that had never come out of his mouth suddenly poured forth. "I know this, because I joined them."

He let go of her hands, pushed himself off the bed and grabbed his pants, pulling them on. "I can't tell you why. I was young, stupid and really, really angry."

"Of course you were," she murmured behind him.

"I overheard my adoptive mother talking once about how the state had asked her and my adoptive dad to take Joe in as well as Danny and I. And she'd refused because he had emotional problems." He ran his fingers through his hair, laughing bitterly. "Yeah, well so did Danny and I. They just weren't visible until later on.

"Joe stopped speaking after our parents were killed. The day they took him away, they said he was going for a drive, but Danny and I knew. We were screaming, crying for him to come back, but they took him away, and he wouldn't even say goodbye."

He turned back to face Sadie, who was watching him with sad eyes. "Rotten story, huh? But none of it is an excuse."

He closed his eyes, remembering, a tremor going through his body. "I was really good at jacking cars, so that's what I did. I jacked cars. I turned a blind eye to the drugs and I drank my ass off. Every damn day. I watched them deal, I watched them pull little kids into the Cobras, teach them how to be violent, get them hooked on smack, and I didn't do a damn thing.

And when some rival gang member did anything to insult us, like set foot in our territory or look at someone's girl the wrong way, we'd all go with our guns and knives into their neighborhood and just start shooting. I carried blanks in my gun, and somehow I thought that made it all okay." He laughed bitterly. "What kind of person does smack like that, Sadie? What kind of person just sits back and watches when other people die?"

She didn't say anything, just waited for him to continue.

"Sonia Sanchez was my girlfriend. She was beautiful, a straight-A student. She wanted to be a doctor." His mouth twisted as he thought of Sonia the woman for the first time in years, rather than Sonia the dead, bleeding corpse.

"Only one thing wrong with her. She loved the idea of my being in a gang. I tried to talk her out of joining, but she went to the Cobra leader behind my back." He swallowed, unable to continue for a moment. "He agreed to let her in if she completed a beating in initiation. Which meant all senior Cobras would hit her as hard as we could for as long as the King Cobra gave us permission."

He heard Sadie's sharp intake of breath, heard it, and hated himself for shocking her. But when he stole a glance at her, bracing himself for the revulsion he knew he'd see there, he still saw only concern.

"There was one Cobra there the day of her initiation who had asked her out, and she'd turned him down. Because she wanted me." He shook his head. "Who knows why. He had a piece of glass. He cut her."

He made a fist, squeezing it with the other hand, staring down at his fingers. "I tried to stop the initiation when I heard. But it's hard to stop thirty-five sober men hell-bent on watching or participating in an initiation rite when you're wasted out of your mind."

"What happened?" Sadie asked softly.

"He killed her. And they all just left me there screaming, with my hand on her neck trying to stop the bleeding. The cops came a few hours later, and I was still sitting there, watching her. That's all I ever did was watch. If I'd just gotten out when she'd first mentioned joining, she'd be alive." He turned away from her, walked to the window and stared out at the expanse of moonlight-tipped grass below. "Stay away from me, Sadie. Everyone who gets too close gets hurt, and I'm usually the one doing the hurting."

He heard her rise behind him, walk to him. And then her arms wrapped around his waist, her cheek lay against his back, between his shoulder blades. They remained like that for several moments, and then she moved around him so that she stood beside him, facing him.

"I couldn't stay away if I tried. I wouldn't want to," she said. "Patricio, what happened to you would have wrecked most people, and you still came through it. You and Danny and Joe. Your parents would be proud of you."

With a derisive laugh, he shook his head, closed his eyes.

"No." She reached up to touch his chin, her gentle touch forcing him to turn to face her, to look at her. "You went through more horror and pain before you were ten than so many people experience in a lifetime," she said. "Yes, you made some bad choices as you dealt with it, but who wouldn't? You survived. You did your best to save Sonia. And you're a good person, Patricio. I know this."

He could only stare at her.

"I can't even pretend to know how you felt," she continued, "how you still feel. But do something for me. Remember that Sonia made her own decision, as did the man who killed her. Remember your parents, remember how much they loved you." She reached out, put her hand over his heart. "Remember this."

He took a deep shuddering breath, closed his eyes, feeling like he'd shatter into a thousand pieces if he so much as looked at her.

"I know you can't forget the past," she said, "but you can let it go, Patricio. Let it go before it consumes you." He felt her rise up, brush a soft kiss on his lips. "Remember this," she said again. "Remember I love you, and you're worth being loved."

Blindly, he reached out, pulling her toward him, clinging to her as if he were a drowning man. And he didn't let her go until the sun came up.

WHEN SADIE WOKE up the next morning, Patricio was gone, and Julio and Ren had no idea where he'd gone—or, if they did, they weren't telling her. He'd left no note, hadn't woken her up to say goodbye. She had no idea whether he was coming back, or whether he simply planned to disappear from her life for good.

She supposed she really ought to congratulate herself. Somewhere in the short time she'd known Patricio, she'd managed to get over her fear of reaching out to other people. Sure, every time she did so, she risked being hurt, but she knew now what could happen when you let yourself go, too.

Patricio had given her an amazing gift, showing her what life was like when you shut yourself off and hid behind old hurts, and simultaneously showing her how wondrous it could be when you let yourself go. And now, she wasn't going to hide from anything. Maybe she'd risk a few embarrassing media stories, a few petty betrayals. But she'd get over it. That's what true friends and a good publicist were for. So no matter what happened with Patricio, she'd be fine. She knew it.

It would just hurt like crazy if he decided she wasn't worth it.

But it was out of her hands—he had to choose whether to hang on to all of that old pain and hurt or whether to let it go and start all over again with her. Because she knew, she *knew* he cared about her, at least a little.

What she didn't know was what he'd do about it. And waiting for him to decide was one of the hardest things she'd ever done.

Sadie went to work as usual, but the lack of sleep combined with her uncanny knack for flashing back to thoughts of Patricio at the most inopportune moments made her performance less than stellar.

"Locke, you suck," Bobby yelled, abruptly ending the fourth take of a scene between her and Jack that she would have nailed any other day. "Go take a break, and we'll shoot around you. And get makeup to do something about those bags under your eyes."

Jack turned away from Bobby and grimaced, then winked at her. He really was a good guy, despite his oddities, and a good friend.

"Donohue, you suck, too," Bobby snapped. He stomped onto the permanent set for Jada Winthrop's university office, waving them away like they were a pair of stray puppies. "Get outta here, both of you." Then, he spun around, yelling at the first crew member he lay eyes on, all frenetic energy and irritation. "Where's Don? Let's do the scene where he comes to the university. And where's my ginger ale? Didn't I ask that intern to get me a ginger ale sometime last week?"

Sadie walked off the set, Jack by her side. As soon as she reached her dressing room door, Meghan was there.

"You okay?" she asked, following Sadie inside, clutching her usual pile of Sadie's urgent mail to her chest. "That's not like you. Bobby never tells you you suck. Now Jack is another story…."

Julio melted out of a shadowy corner where he'd apparently been working on his invisibility skills, coming to stand just outside her door. Sadie greeted him and went inside with Meghan. "I'm fine. Thanks for asking," she said.

"And where's Patricio?" Meghan looked over her shoulder at the closed dressing room door, behind which Julio was standing. Placing the mail on the vanity table to her left, she sat sideways in Sadie's makeup chair, leaning her arm on top of the chair's back.

"He's gone," Sadie said. "That's Julio, and the tall half-Japanese guy running around is Ren. They're two of the associates in Rodriguez and Associates." She blew a stray lock of hair out of her eyes and slumped down in the chair. "Meghan, I have a question for you, and I'd appreciate it if you answered honestly."

"Sure, boss," Meghan answered, her face serious. "What's up?"

"Do you enjoy your job?" Sadie bit her

lip, wondering whether there was another way to put the question to get at the information she was seeking. "I haven't been a jerk to you, have I?"

Meghan laughed, her red curls bouncing as she shook her head. "Jeez, no! You've been great. I love working for you. The hours are good, my workload is fun, and you never scream at me if your bottled water isn't at room temperature. It's just…" She bit her bottom lip, letting the sentence trail off.

"What? It's just what?" When Meghan didn't respond, Sadie prompted her again. "It's okay. I asked for honesty, remember?"

"Well," Meghan began reluctantly. "I mean, I know I'm your employee and we're not supposed to be friends, but you could…" She twirled her hand in the air, fishing for the right words. "Lighten up a little. I know you've had some jerks working for you in the past, but I swear, I'm not going to sell your secrets to the highest bidder."

Sadie picked at a stray thread on the chair's upholstery, considering her assistant's words. "I know you're not," she said, and to her surprise, she really meant it. "And you know, you're probably the closest person I have to a friend right now," she said quietly.

Meghan was quiet for a moment, and when Sadie finally got the courage to steal a look at her, she saw Meghan was smiling. "Well, then we can be unprofessional together, because you're the closest person I have to a friend, here, too." She scooted her chair forward, so she was sitting closer to Sadie. "Now, since that's out of the way, tell me everything about Patricio."

Sadie laughed incredulously. "What do you think I'd have to tell?"

Meghan tapped her cheek, looking up at the ceiling. "Oh, let's see. Hot bodyguard who not only can't take his eyes off you—"

"Uh, that's his job," Sadie pointed out.

Meghan ignored her. "But he looks like he wants to have you for breakfast most of the time."

"He does not."

"Now he's gone, and you lose all ability to concentrate. And there is zero sexual tension between you and Julio," Meghan said. "Which leads me to believe there's some behind the scenes drama going on. Now, spill. If you can't confide in me, who can you confide in?"

Sadie thought for a moment. "This goes nowhere."

"Of course not."

So Sadie told Meghan the whole thing, except for the more personal details about Patricio's past, starting from her first meeting with Patricio to waking up that morning and finding him gone. "I don't know if he's coming back," she said, feeling hollow and sad as she said the words. "And it makes me crazy. I just want to shake him and tell him to just let himself be happy for once."

Meghan sighed sadly. "Yeah, but you can't decide that for him. You know," she said, perking up in her chair. "Cary and I were going to pop in a movie tonight and work on answering some of your fan mail. You should come over. If he does come back, you'll at least look like you aren't wallowing."

Sadie considered the invitation. It sounded almost perfect—low-key and it would keep her from dwelling too much on what she couldn't control. Except... "I don't want to be a third wheel."

"*Pffft.*" Meghan flipped a hand at her. "Cary won't care. He's just trying to help me get this done so we can have a nice night out tomorrow."

"Well, in that case, why don't you bring the mailing to my house? You can stay over in one of the guest rooms, if you want," she said. "That way, I don't have to drag Julio and Ren into your house."

Meghan nodded. "Good idea. We'd be tripping all over each other at my apartment. Deal."

Sadie's cell phone buzzed, vibrating on the vanity table where she'd left it. She lunged for it, her heart hammering.

Meghan gripped the chair back. "Is it Patricio?" she mouthed even before Sadie could flip open her phone.

"Hello?" she said once she'd done so.

"Hello, Sadie."

It wasn't Patricio.

"Who is this?" she asked. But she knew.

"Thank you for wearing blue today. You know it's my favorite color," the caller said.

Sadie looked over at the blue silk shirt she'd worn to the studio today, hanging on a bar near her dressing room door. Oh, God, he'd been close enough to see her....

"Who is he, Sadie?" the man said casually.

"I don't know what you're talking about," she replied.

"Yes, you do," he said. "You know very well who I'm talking about. He's not good enough for you, Sadie." The man's voice grew louder. "Not good enough for you to be whoring yourself for him."

She inhaled sharply. What had he seen? How did he know?

"Slut," he hissed. "You think I don't see the way you flaunt yourself in front of him? I worshiped you. I treated you like a queen, and instead of appreciating all I've done for you, you turn your back on us."

"There is no us," she snapped. The door clicked open, and Sadie looked up to see

Meghan leading Julio into the room, concern written all over her features. "It's in your head. I want you to leave me alone and never approach me or call me again."

He started laughing, a derisive, mocking sound. "Oh, no, sweetheart. It doesn't work that way. "We're meant to be." And then his voice turned into a conspiratorial whisper. "Do you know what happened to the last woman who rejected me?"

Clutching the small phone tightly, Sadie refused to answer. She wouldn't give him the satisfaction, but she knew. Oh, how she knew.

"I don't want to have to do that to you, Sadie." Now his voice was pleading. "I love you. And you love me. You just forgot. I'll come for you tonight. I'll make you remember."

"I don't," she responded firmly. "I don't love you, and I want you to leave me alone."

There was silence. It stretched out for what seemed like ages, though she could hear his heavy, gasping breaths on the other end of the line.

"Be careful what you wish for," he

snapped suddenly. "Because you'd have to die for me to do that." And then he broke the connection.

Chapter Twelve

When Patricio entered the Southern California Women's Facility visitor's room, Amelia Allen was waiting for him.

His footsteps echoed on the tiled floor as he crossed the room toward where she sat, at the same table at which she'd been seated the last time he'd seen her. Unlike that previous visit, he'd come alone this time.

She gave him a placid smile when he pulled out the chair across from her, the legs squealing in protest. Patricio sat down.

"Why, Detective Rodriguez, how lovely to see you again," she said, as if he'd come for tea or something.

"I'm not Detective Rodriguez," he said, softly so the guards couldn't hear. "I'm Patricio."

Her eyes narrowed, and she pushed back from the table in protest.

He held up a hand to stop her from alerting the guards, from leaving. "Mrs. Allen, please. I'm not here to hurt you or even to yell at you. I lost it last time I was here, and I shouldn't have."

Her mouth flattening in disapproval, Amelia blinked at him, folding her arms across the tabletop. He couldn't understand why she was looking at him like he'd committed some hideous social gaffe, seeing as she was a *murderer* and all. But he guessed that she'd somehow managed to bury the reality of her crimes somewhere deep in her subconscious. She probably no more thought herself a murderer than she thought herself an astronaut.

They stared quietly at each other. Patricio had rehearsed the entire scene in his mind all the way here in the car, and now, when it counted, he couldn't find the right words to start the conversation to save his life. Sadie would have known what to say. She would have been right here, by his side, if he'd asked her.

Don't think about Sadie.

"My sister had this crazy laugh," he said, because he wasn't thinking—he was just speaking. And it wasn't according to any plan he'd come in with. "It was this clear, happy sound that seemed to go on forever, and you just had to laugh with her. She was eighteen months old the last time I saw her, and my brothers and I used to have contests to see who could make her laugh first. It was easy."

Amelia pulled her chin back, obviously puzzled by the non sequiturs flying out of his mouth.

"She was a beautiful baby," he continued. "People used to tell us that all the time when we walked with her and our parents down the street. We were happy." He leaned forward. "I miss my parents, Mrs. Allen. I miss my sister."

She didn't say anything, didn't even move. But still he pressed on. Because it was his last chance.

"I'm guessing you didn't have a family like that growing up," Patricio said. "Because if you had, you wouldn't have found it so easy to take mine." He stopped, swallowed and looked away for a moment. "I'm sorry about whatever it was your childhood was lacking. And even though what my father did doesn't come close to taking someone's life, I'm sorry he blackmailed your husband. I'm ashamed of his actions, and every damn day I wish I could ask him why he felt like what we had wasn't enough."

He looked her straight in the eye, wanting her to know he meant every word he was saying. "I'm not asking you for an apology. I don't want one. And I want you to know that when I walk out of here today, I'm going to do my damnedest to forget you. Because I forgive you."

Her brow furrowed, and her mouth dropped open into a small O, but still she didn't say a word. He saw the hand laying on the table tremble slightly. "I forgive you, Amelia. Whether you're even sorry for what happened to my parents or not. I forgive you, and I'm finally putting this behind me. But I'm giving you a chance to move forward today, too, to make something right out of this stupid, stupid situation." He paused. "Tell me where my sister is. Tell me what you know."

She remained silent, her mouth working slightly, as if part of her wanted to tell him but was warring with the part of her that wanted to keep her secrets. He sat there for what seemed like several minutes, willing her with all his energy to speak.

They sat like that until the guard called an end to visiting hours. She wasn't going to talk.

Defeat settled like a rock on his shoulders, but he stood, refusing to let her see that she'd gotten to him once again. He still had Joe and Daniel, and together, they'd find Sabrina, if it took another twenty-five years to do it. But God, he hoped it wasn't that long.

As he turned to go, he heard her clear her throat, mutter something behind him. He went back to the table. "Ma'am?" he said.

She looked up at him, and he could have sworn there were tears in her eyes. "Port Renegade. She went to a family in Port

Renegade, Washington," she said. "Their last name is Adelante."

AFTER TWO home movies, at least one too many glasses of wine, and an obscene amount of popcorn, Sadie rose from the floor where she and Meghan had been addressing fan mail responses. Cary sat above them on the couch, helping out when he could and listening to the girl talk with amusement.

"I'm wiped out. I'm going to bed," she announced.

Meghan stumbled up to stand beside her. "Oooh, my head. That was good wine."

Sadie nodded. "Gift from some millionaire producer guy. Only the best for him." She flung an arm around Meghan. "Thanks, hon. I had a great time."

"Me, too." Meghan put a head on her shoulder. "I'm glad we ran out of wine when we did, or we'd probably be getting to the 'I love you, man,' stage of drunkenness right now."

"And that's never pretty," Sadie agreed. She said good-night to Meghan and her boyfriend and went up to her room, Julio coming up behind them. Ren was in one of the spare bedrooms near hers, taking his turn to sleep.

After an hour or so of reading, Sadie went inside the bathroom adjoining her bedroom to brush her teeth. She heard someone open the door, heard it snick shut behind them. "Meghan?" she called, stepping back into her bedroom.

But it wasn't Meghan; it was Cary standing at the foot of her bed. "Meghan's asleep," he said.

"Cary?" she said, wondering what in the world he was doing there. And then she saw the gun.

"It's David," he said. "Say David. Say my name."

Oh, God. He couldn't be David Carpenter, couldn't be Lovesick. She drew a deep, shuddering breath. She'd stared at the business end of a prop gun so many times as Jada Winthrop, the situation almost didn't seem real. But it was.

He stepped around the bed, raising the gun straight at her heart. It had a silencer.

"David Carpenter. But you can't be. You don't look a thing like your picture," she murmured.

David reached up and stroked his chin with his free hand. "I had a little work done. Hair, cheekbones, colored contacts. I wanted to look my best for you," he said.

"David, what do you want?"

"You, Sadie," he said in a voice that was suddenly all too familiar. "We're meant to be."

She shook her head. "No."

He lashed out, striking her temple with a backhand slap. "Bitch!"

She cried out, holding the side of her face where he'd struck. He stepped forward, cupping her face with his hands and turning her toward him, stroking her cheek with the muzzle of his gun. "I'm sorry," he whispered, looking like he was going to cry. "I'm so sorry. I don't want to hurt you, but you have to understand. You're my soul mate. I won't see you make a whore of yourself with another man."

With that, he gripped her arm, so hard, she was sure he'd left bruises.

"Where's Meghan?" she asked as he propelled her toward the door. She wondered where Ren and Julio were.

"She's fine," he said. "As long as you're good and do what you're told, she'll be fine. She'll have a headache in the morning, and maybe a broken heart." He laughed, opened the door. "She loved me, you know. I'm easy to love. You just have to spend some time with me. You never spend time with me."

He was strong. She tried to stop when she saw Julio sprawled on the floor in her hallway, but David kept her moving. Had he killed them? Where was Ren? What had he done to Meghan?

She considered calling out, trying to wake Ren, but David seemed to read her mind. "You can scream if you want to, but no one will hear you. I drugged your body-guards. They drink a lot of water, and they seem to prefer that cooler in your kitchen. It was easy. Drugged Meghan, too."

They moved down the stairs, and he stopped next to the security keypad. "De-activate it, and don't even think about try-ing anything," he said.

She did as she was told. "Where are we going?"

He smiled. "Somewhere private. Someplace where no one will ever find us, where I can have you to myself." He put a hand on the back of her head and pulled her face roughly toward him, planting a harsh kiss on her lips.

Breathing heavily with barely contained panic, she looked around her, trying to figure out her options. Because enough people had told her that once a criminal got you to a secondary location he was familiar with, where he felt in complete control, you were as good as dead.

And David had killed before.

She could pretend to be in love with him, but she didn't know how long she could keep up the charade, especially if they went where no one could find him. She couldn't even keep it together for a kiss. She'd rather die than let him go further.

After she'd deactivated the alarm, he pulled her outside, to a small convertible. He started unlocking the passenger side, and she noticed something sticking out of the back pocket of his Dockers. Like a Swiss Army knife. Sadie wondered if she'd have a chance to get that away from him.

He spun around abruptly. "Get into the trunk."

She gasped in horror. Small, enclosed, dark places terrified her. And the trunk of his tiny car didn't look like it would fit a child, much less a grown woman.

He hit a button on his key chain, and the trunk lid rose. "Get in!" he shouted.

He released her momentarily to point to the wide, black maw of the trunk, just waiting for her. Taking advantage of her fleeting freedom, she made a break for it.

She'd only run a few feet away before she felt something hit her in the small of the back with incredible force. She fell to the ground, and then he was on top of her. Gripping a handful of her hair, he pulled her head back. And then, to her horror, the knife was at her throat.

"I'll cut you right here, bitch, leave you to die in your front yard like an animal," he snarled.

She whimpered. She couldn't help it. She was so angry and so frustrated. She didn't want to die at the hands of a horrible man like him. Tears of anger ran down her face. And then she thought of Patricio.

He'd blame himself for her death.

She forced herself to relax, determined to fight to her last breath, determined to survive. "I'm sorry, David," she said, making her voice as docile as possible.

With a grunt of satisfaction, he pulled her up by her arm, shoving her against the back end of the car. He waited until she was inside, and then he slammed the lid shut.

The sound of her own breathing seemed to echo inside her ears as the dark wrapped around her like a suffocating blanket. She heard the engine rumble to life and she lurched backward as the car backed out of its parking spot near her house. And then they were driving, headed for heaven knew where.

Somewhere isolated. Somewhere dark.

They turned left at the end of her driveway, and then another right, which probably put them on Wilshire. No doubt he'd head for one of the highways, and then get them out of town. If she could keep her bearings, she might be able to figure out where they were headed.

But did it really matter? She kicked the trunk lid as hard as her limited movement would allow. It didn't give an inch.

The taillights.

A fleeting memory came back to her, of a self-defense instructor telling her that if she was ever thrown into the trunk of the car to kick out the taillights. She could stick her hand through the opening and wave at anyone driving behind them, who would no doubt know that something was seriously wrong as soon as he or she realized there was a body in the trunk of the car ahead.

She went to work, feeling the interior of the car, finding a tangle of metal and wires that told her she'd located the light. And then she started ripping at it with her hands, pulling and shoving and hitting it until she'd knocked the light out of the car. Cool air rushed into the trunk through the opening, and she could see only a smattering of lights behind her. There were no cars, and it looked like they were headed out of the city.

Refusing to give up, Sadie stuck her hand through the opening and waved with all of her might.

A COUPLE OF hours later, her hand exhausted from trying to signal cars behind them, Sadie heard the car tires crunch on gravel. A couple of times, she thought she'd seen a car behind them without lights, but then she'd look again and conclude that it was just wishful thinking. She wondered if anyone had seen her, if anyone had alerted the police.

Judging by the lack of cars and sirens within eye- and earshot, she doubted it.

She peered through the hole and saw that they were approaching a couple of warehouselike buildings, their interior windows dark. A few large piles of gravel towered over a couple pieces of construction equipment, leading her to the conclusion that they were approaching either a gravel pit or a highway construction crew's garage.

Either way, there didn't appear to be anyone around.

The car stopped, and she heard a car door slam.

Finally the trunk popped open, and David looked down at her. He reached in and hauled her out by the neckline of her shirt, his handsome face twisted in an expression of fury that even the darkness couldn't hide.

"Thought you could signal for help?" he asked. He wrapped his hands around her throat, stroking the hollow between her collarbones with his thumbs. "Too bad no one saw you."

He kissed her again, and this time, she retched as soon as his lips touched hers. "I know you love me."

She shook her head. "I don't, David. You can't make someone love you."

He laughed softly, a low, ominous sound. "I can."

She felt the knife before she saw it, drawing a line down her skin as he cut her flimsy camisole from collar to navel. Blood beaded up on the shallow cut he'd made on her skin. "Before the night is over," he whispered, "you will love me."

Sadie was about to reply when she saw movement in the shadows along the narrow gravel road they'd taken to the warehouse. But when she looked again, there was nothing there. Perhaps there never had been.

Patricio, please.

She swallowed, looked at the man before her. "You're hurting me, David."

"You hurt me," he bit back, his face so close to hers, she could feel his breath. There was no alcohol on it—he hadn't had any wine. He reached up and slammed the trunk lid shut, pushed her back against it. He motioned for her to sit on the trunk, and when she had, he pushed her with one hand so she was lying back.

"I'll make you remember you love me." He grabbed her knee, pushing it outward. When she tried to sit back up, he brought the knife to her neck once more. She held still. God, it was so dark and so quiet. So damned quiet, telling her there wasn't another soul around for miles. Whatever he'd do to her, he'd do without anyone hearing her scream.

He moved to stand between her spread knees, his hand stroking her leg. "We're meant to be," he said.

"I don't think so," a voice said behind him.

Patricio.

Sadie saw a pair of hands grip David by the shoulders, and then David swung away from her like a rag doll. She sat up, just in time to see David's knife fly toward her to land in the gravel at her feet.

Patricio punched David quickly in the stomach, causing the man to double over as he expelled his breath in an "oof." Before David could rise, Patricio kneed him in the face, and when his head snapped back, Patricio delivered a backhand chop to his left temple. David lurched to the side, and, letting momentum carry his arm to the right, Patricio swung his hand back and hit David on the right side of his face.

David stumbled again, circling clumsily to the left. It appeared that Patricio would easily subdue the man, until David reached back and pulled something out of the back of his jeans.

His gun.

Patricio went still.

David swiped at his mouth with his free hand, the other aiming the gun straight at Patricio's heart.

Oh, no. God, please, no.

"You're going to die now, you freaking spic," David snarled. "And then I'm going to have Sadie a hundred different ways before I kill her, too. She's not worthy of me."

Patricio shook his head. "You've got it wrong, David. You're not worthy of her. But I am." He took a step forward.

David pulled the trigger.

Patricio jerked back, and Sadie screamed but he was still on his feet. The shot had gone wild. Thank God. She bent down, scooping up the knife, moving toward David.

"You'll never be worthy of her," Patricio continued. "And I'm not the one who's going to die tonight." He moved forward in a lightning-fast movement, scissoring his arms in front of him. He caught David's outstretched wrist neatly between his two hands, and the gun went flying. So did Sadie's knife.

The blade caught David in the shoulder, and he screamed as the knife severed the nerves of his arm, causing it to hang useless at his side. Patricio drew back and delivered a punch to his chin, and he crumpled unconscious to the ground. Patricio picked him up and dumped him in the trunk of his own car, slamming the lid closed.

Then he turned to Sadie, and she was in his arms.

"Patricio, how did you…?" She clung to him, unable to finish her own question, she was so choked by emotion and relief and a pure, strong love for him.

She pulled away from him, and he let her go easily. Too easily. But maybe the fact that he'd held her just before was enough. In the distance, she could hear sirens approaching.

'Meghan." The thought of what David Carpenter might have done to her assistant made her feel sick. "Ren and Julio. Patricio, I don't know…"

Before she could finish, he was dialing his cell phone. After a few minutes of conversation, he hung up. "That was Danny," he explained. "They're all fine. A little out of it, but the EMTs say that'll wear off."

"Thank God," she breathed.

He nodded.

"How long?"

"Since you came home from work," he responded. "I couldn't get to you in time before he put you in the trunk, so I followed you." He looked away, obviously uneasy.

"And you're blaming yourself because you weren't right there? Are you high? You saved my life." She reached out, cupping his cheek. "You saved my life again."

He grimaced, his eyes looking down at something other than her. But she refused to let him go, to back away. "And I think you feel something, at least a little of what I feel for you."

He looked up at her then, his body unmoving.

"It's okay if you can't say it or do anything about it," she said. "I just wanted you to hear that I know. And if you decide to take a chance, I'll be here." She laughed softly. "I'd like to tell you that as an independent woman of the twenty-first century I won't be waiting around for you to make up your mind, but I think it's going to take me a long, long time to get over you, Patricio Rodriguez." She stepped forward and stood on her toes, kissing him softly on the cheek. "You saved my life," she whispered against his skin. "You are the strongest, best man I know. And whether you think so or not, I know you well."

She started to back away when his arms snapped up to catch her, to keep her from leaving him. "I am so in love with you," he said into her hair. He took a deep, shuddering breath, blew it out as he wrapped his arms around her. "I think I fell in love when you threw that knife at my head." He bent down, so his forehead was touching hers. "You're beautiful, inside and out, and I want to spend the rest of my life trying to be like you." He kissed her then, so tenderly it took her breath away. "I love you, Sadie Locke. I can't promise I'll be perfect. I can't tell you I've worked through all this crap in my head, but I've started. And it's because of you."

She reached up and put her arms around his neck, tears in her eyes.

"You saved me," he breathed against her lips, then kissed her again. "And I will love you the best I can for the rest of my life if you'll let me."

He touched her cheek, and she placed a hand over his, trying to commit every bit of this moment to memory so she could hold it forever. As the police cars turned down the road, approaching them, she saw him smile at her, a slow, private smile. "Then what else do we need?" she said.

Epilogue

Being the one who could easily gain the trust of the people inside with one show of his badge, Daniel stepped forward, Joe and Patricio on either side, waiting.

The three of them stared at the door.

Taking a deep breath, Daniel squared his shoulders. "Ready?" he asked.

"Yeah, sure," Patricio said briskly, just before Joe's quick, "Uh-huh." All three brothers pretended they were fine, that this was an average visit on an average day. That their hearts weren't going to be broken if Sabrina Adelante wasn't the woman they thought she was.

Daniel rang the doorbell.

Joe shoved his hands in his pockets and stared at his shuffling feet. Patricio rubbed his chin with one hand, ignoring his racing pulse.

"Just a second," a female voice called. They could hear her footsteps approaching.

What if it wasn't her?

The door swung open, and a tiny woman with dark brown eyes and strawberry-blond hair stood before them, a red maternity T-shirt covering her protruding belly.

Patricio saw Danny's shoulders sink with disappointment, heard Joe's defeated sigh. But he refused to let go of that damned optimism Sadie had drummed into his head. The pieces had all fallen into place this time, and they'd checked and double-checked every lead that had brought them to this doorstep. Maybe the woman wasn't Sabrina. Maybe she was a friend. Hell, maybe they had an Irish ancestor who'd given Ramon and Daniela Lopez recessive genes for reddish-blond hair. Whatever the case, he wasn't going to let his hopes flag until he knew for sure this wasn't their lost sister.

"Sabrina Adelante?" he asked behind Daniel. His words caused Daniel to blink, shake himself back out of whatever thoughts he'd been preoccupied with.

The woman looked at each of the brothers, one hand on her belly, the other on the door frame. "Who wants to know?"

Daniel pulled out his badge. "I'm Detective Daniel Rodriguez with the LAPD, and these are my brothers, Joe and Patricio."

"I'm her sister, Casey," the woman said, her eyes widening slightly at the mention of the LAPD. "Is everything okay?"

"Everything's fine, ma'am," Daniel said quickly. "We were just… I mean…" He trailed off, and Daniel and Joe didn't step in to help him. They'd been so preoccupied with finding Sabrina, with seeing her at least once, that none of them had considered how they'd explain their presence, their shared history. God, maybe they'd made a mistake.

None of them noticed when a tall, athleticlooking woman walked up behind Casey, not until she was standing in the small space in the doorway beside her. Patricio was the first to notice her.

"Sabrina." Her name came out on a sigh. The eyes were the same striking light brown as his own. She had the same glossy black hair, which was tied back in a ponytail, much like their mother had worn hers in nearly every one of his memories of her. In fact, with her straight nose, high cheekbones, and square jaw, Sabrina was the spitting image of Daniela Lopez.

"Can I help...?" She blinked, stepped forward. She looked at Patricio, really looked at him for several seconds. His throat tightened, and he couldn't have spoken if he'd tried. Their baby sister. She looked happy. She looked blessed.

Then her focus went to Daniel. She studied him silently. "Twins," she whispered under her breath. And she turned to Joe. "You look like me," she said, an expression of wonder on her face. Behind her, Casey started in surprise, then, after taking another look at the brothers, crept quietly into the house.

Joe nodded. "Sabrina," he choked out.

Bringing her hands together as if she were praying, she held them in front of her mouth and just looked at all three of them again. "We're related, aren't we?" she asked from behind her fingers.

Daniel regained his composure first. "You're our sister," he said. "Our baby sister."

"We've been looking for you for a long time," Joe added.

"Wow," she breathed. "Brothers." Sabrina reached out with one hand for Patricio, the brother nearest her. She placed a palm on his upper chest, as if assuring herself that she wasn't seeing things when she looked at him. Still touching him, she put her other palm on Danny's arm, connecting them. "There's only been Casey and me. I always wondered what it would be like…"

And then she let the twins go and stepped toward Joe, taking the lapels of his leather jacket in both hands. Leaning forward, she closed her eyes and inhaled deeply, a contented smile on her face. Then she straightened, a question in her amber eyes. "I know this is going to sound ridiculous, but that seems familiar. The smell of this jacket. But it can't…"

Joe gave her a crooked smile. "Meguiar's leather cleaner. Papi bought me a leather jacket when I was nine on the condition that I take good care of it. He swore on the stuff."

She bent down and smelled Joe again. And then, suddenly, she wrapped her arms around his waist, holding him close, burying her face in his chest. Taken aback, Joe's hands shot up in the air in surprise, but it didn't take him long to put his arms around his sister.

When Sabrina lifted her head, her eyes were shining. "Oh, man, I'm a mess." Laughing, she swiped at her eye with the heel of one hand, still clinging to Joe with the other. "When I was little, I used to ask my mother where my brothers were. It's like I always knew you were out there," she said. And then she reached out, pulling Daniel first and then Patricio into her embrace, which somehow had become wide enough to encompass them all.

"We missed you," Danny said. "So much."

They remained like that for several minutes, and then Sabrina pulled back to look at them all again. "I assume our parents died for them to split us up like this," she said carefully. At Joe's nod, she continued. "Are there more of us? More in the family, I mean?"

Danny shook his head. "No. We're it. Sorry."

At that, she threw her head back and laughed, a loud, musical, exuberant laugh that still had something in it that reminded Patricio of what she'd sounded like laughing as a baby. She reached forward and cupped Danny's face. "Don't be sorry. This is amazing." She took her hand away quickly. "Is that too much, too soon? I've always been a touchy-feely person, but...."

Danny reached for her, pulling her into another embrace. "Not at all," he rasped.

When she let him go, Patricio smacked Danny lightly in the back of the head with his fingertips.

"Hey!" Danny said as he spun around.

"You forgot the wives, dude," Patricio informed him. "Celia would have your head if she heard you."

Danny rubbed the back of his head, scowling good-naturedly at his twin. "She meant blood relations, loser."

"You're married?" Sabrina asked.

"These two are." Patricio indicated Joe

and Daniel. "I'm, uh, engaged." He glanced back at the van they'd rented. "Sadie's probably going to ask you to be in the wedding. I hope you don't mind." When she didn't say anything right away, he echoed her previous words. "Too much, too soon?"

She grinned, squeezed his elbow, looking back at him with his mother's eyes. "I'd be honored." And then she looked past him at the van. "Are they here? Can I meet them?"

Without another word, Joe ran back to the van to get the women. As soon as he opened the door, Emma, Celia and Sadie nearly trampled over him to stampede toward Sabrina, their speech a cacophony of "It's her?" and "Oh, my God" and "Look at her eyes."

Sabrina cocked an eyebrow at Patricio. "You're engaged to Sadie Locke?" He nodded. "Shut up!"

The rest of their conversation was cut off as Celia, Emma and Sadie swarmed onto the porch, catching Sabrina in their arms. And when all the tears and hugs were done, they went inside, a complete family at last.

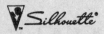

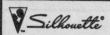

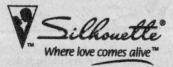